Sharp

Also by Dominic Barker published by Catnip
Sharp Stuff

Sharp Beats

Dominic Barker

CATNIP BOOKS
Published by Catnip Publishing Ltd.
14 Greville Street
London EC1N 8SB

This edition published 2009
1 3 5 7 9 10 8 6 4 2

A CIP catalogue record for this book is available from the British
Library

ISBN 978-1-84647-051-6

Printed in Poland

www.catnippublishing.co.uk

CHAPTER 1

'DUM. DA DA DUM. DA DA DUM. DA DA DUM'
　There's a drum outside my shed.
'DA DA DUM. DA DA DUM. DA DA DUM.'
　And a bass.
'DA DA DUM. DA DA DUM.'
　It's moving and it's getting louder.
'DA DA DUM.'
　The door opens.
'DA DA DUM. DA DA DUM. DA DA DUM.'
　Whatever this is I want to meet it standing up. I shoot out of my chair and send my can of coke flying across my desk. I dive and catch it just in time. Which is a good thing – it's my last one.
　The beat stops.
　I look round.
　There's three other people in my shed. A girl and two boys. They are all wearing these big puffa jackets even though it's not cold or anything. One of the boys has just switched off some kind of fancy mobile which has been pushing out the beats. He must have had it

supercharged or something because it's really loud.

'Hey!'

The girl pulls a newspaper from inside his jacket and smacks it down on my desk.

'This you?' she demands.

I look down at the paper. There's a big circle around my advert:

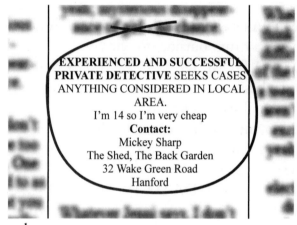

EXPERIENCED AND SUCCESSFUL PRIVATE DETECTIVE SEEKS CASES
ANYTHING CONSIDERED IN LOCAL AREA.
I'm 14 so I'm very cheap
Contact:
Mickey Sharp
The Shed, The Back Garden
32 Wake Green Road
Hanford

I nod.

'You any good?' she demands.

I decide that this isn't the time for understatement.

'I'm the best,' I tell her.

'You'd better be,' she says. 'Because we've got a problem. And we need it solved quick. Now, listen up because I ain't got time to repeat myself.'

Everything is happening way quicker than it usually does. I scramble in the desk drawer for a pencil and a notebook.

'You know who we are, right?' she assumes.

I don't have a clue.

'Er…remind me?'

'We're the Really Tough Crew,' she tells me. 'We're the biggest thing in Hanford right now. We're putting out a groundbreaking fusion of UK Garage, R'n'B and Hip Hop. This here is DJ MC Hassle who lays down the beats.' She points to the black guy holding the fancy phone. 'This is Spider who does the keyboard, computer multi-tracking and sampling.' She points to the white guy who despite his big jacket actually looks quite weedy. 'And I'm Jenni. I do the rapping.'

'Now I remember,' I say. If a client thinks they are the biggest thing in Hanford then it can't do any harm to agree.'

'So, you've got an idea about our problem then,' she says.

Maybe it wasn't such a good idea.

'Er…remind me again,' I say.

She shakes her head.

'We've got a demo session in a recording studio on Saturday. If we do well then maybe we could get a record deal.'

'Congratulations,' I tell her.

'Congratulations, nothing,' she snaps back. 'What good is a recording session when Desiree's vanished?'

'Who's Desiree?'

'Desiree's our singer. So we've got somebody to do the beats and me to do the raps but nobody to sing.'

'Why don't you sing the chorus?' I suggest.

'I'm a rapper.' Jenni's lip curls as she answers me. 'I don't sing.'

'Right,' I agree quickly because it seems a touchy subject. 'What about somebody else?'

'Who?' she says.

'I don't know,' I tell her. 'There must be another singer in Hanford.'

There's kind of an angry mumble from all three of them when I say that.

'You don't get it, do you?' Jenni says. 'Desiree's the best singer I've ever heard. She's Aretha and Whitney rolled into one. She's on the CD we sent to the record company and they're going to want to hear her when we get there to lay down a demo.'

'Okay,' I say. 'But even a singer who isn't as good must be better than no singer at all.'

'I keep talking but I guess you can't be listening,' Jenni tells me. 'We don't want no stringy wannabee who messes up all the high stuff by wailing like a dying animal because she thinks it shows she's got feelings. We want Desiree. And we want you to find her and get her to that session. You got a problem with that?'

I shake my head.

'Good,' Jenni tells me. 'She didn't show up to

practice two days ago. I phoned her and I texted her but I didn't get no answer. That's really strange because she never misses a practice and she always turns up on time. She loves singing. That's all she does.'

'Did you go round to her house when she didn't phone you back?' I ask.

'Course I did. You think I'm dumb or something?' Jenni is one touchy girl. You ask her a question and she thinks it's an insult. 'I went round her house the next day. Her mum came to the door and I say 'Where's Desiree?' and she says she don't know and I says 'You're her mother. You should know. What kind of parent do you think you are?' and then she got really angry and slammed the door in my face.'

I'm not surprised. Telling adults that they're lousy parents is never a good idea. They all think that they're the best parents in the world even when they're really obviously not. Like my dad. When he's had a couple of glasses of whisky he's always saying he's given me and Karen, my sister, a really good upbringing when half the time he can't even remember to give us any pocket money. Imagine forgetting something as basic as that and still thinking that you're doing a good job. It's like being a fireman and forgetting to turn the tap on your hosepipe.

'Look,' I say, taking a deep breath because I've got a feeling that Jenni isn't going to like what I've got to say, 'It doesn't sound like we can even be sure that

Desiree's vanished. Just because she doesn't answer her phone and then you go and upset her mum doesn't prove anything.'

'Do you want this case or not?' she says. 'Because you're acting like you don't.'

She's got a point there. It's one of my problems. I forget that I should do all the negotiations about pay and expenses and stuff before I start thinking about the case.

'I do want it,' I tell her, 'but I want to make sure that there is a case before I start investigating. I don't want to waste your money for nothing.'

I'm pleased with that. It makes me sound like the kind of guy people can trust. Which I am. Mostly.

'Don't you worry about that,' Jenni tells me. 'You just worry about finding her and getting her there. Right?'

I nod.

Then I take a swallow. This is the bit I always find the hardest – asking for money.

'I charge ten pounds a day plus expenses,' I tell them. It's more than I normally ask for but I figure that if they get a record deal then they're going to be really rich and so ten pounds a day won't mean nothing to them.

'You got a deal,' she says. 'Ten pounds a day plus expenses.'

This has never happened before. Normally my clients argue about how much I'm charging.

'I'll need a picture of her and her address and mobile and your address and mobile.'

Jenni writes the addresses down and adds the mobile numbers.

'I'll get a photo to you tomorrow,' she says. 'Come on, Crew.'

The boys head out the shed. Jenni stops by the door and turns back.

'We need you to get Desiree to that demo session,' she says. 'You understand?

I nod.

'Remember,' says Jenni, 'She's real pretty but she's dumb. That's a dangerous combination.'

CHAPTER 2

Whatever Jenni says, I don't think that it's going to be too difficult to find Desiree. One of the things you get used to as a teenage detective is that you aren't going to get the really exciting cases. Bullying – yeah; stolen trophy – yeah; dodgy Head Boy election – yeah; mysterious disappearance of cat – yeah; mysterious disappearance of girl – no chance. Cases like that go straight to the police. Which I don't think is necessarily fair but it's the way it is.

The mistake Jenni made was looking at things just from her own point of view. When you're an experienced and successful detective like I am you learn that there's more than one way to look at things. Take Jenni. What she did was to add three things together – Desiree missing practice and not answering her phone and her mum not knowing where she was – and she came up with the answer that Desiree must have vanished. That might make a bit of sense if you look at it from Jenni's angle but it makes no sense at all if you look at it like you were Desiree's mum.

Imagine you were Desiree's mum and you didn't know where Desiree was and then her best friend knocks on your door and says she doesn't know where Desiree is either and that she's not answering her phone. You wouldn't get into an argument with Desiree's best friend. You'd panic and start saying 'Oh my God, Oh my God. I've got to call the police.' But Desiree's mum doesn't do that so I figure that, even though she didn't know where Desiree was right at that moment, she still knew that she hadn't vanished or anything, and if Jenni hadn't been so rude to her right off Desiree's mum probably would have told her that. But it doesn't take more than one minute with Jenni to know that she argues first and asks questions later.

So, having worked it all out logically, I nip inside my house check nobody's about and phone Desiree. Straight to voice mail so at least Jenni was right about something. I get on my bike and head over to Desiree's house. I figure I'm going to have this case solved without even needing to see her photograph.

I almost don't get there though. It's raining and it's that time when it's not really day any more but it's not really dark yet. The main roads are all jammed up with cars because everybody is coming home from work. I guess they can't be seeing things too good because I nearly get run over three times.

I check out Desiree's house. It's normal. Windows

and doors and stuff. There must be somebody in because there's a light on in the front room although I can't see who because the curtains are closed. But I'm sure it's Desiree. I don't know why exactly. But I know it is. Detectives get this feeling sometimes. It's called a hunch. It shows that you're a proper detective when you get one so I'm quite pleased about it. And the one rule about hunches is that you have to follow them. So, I wheel my bike up the drive and knock firmly on the front door.

A dog starts barking. Footsteps get nearer. The door opens.

'Yeah?'

The person who opens the door is definitely not Desiree. It's a man and he doesn't look friendly.

'What d'you want?'

His question is followed by a big growl. His dog is behind him and he doesn't look too friendly either.

'I'm looking for Desiree,' I blurt.

If all else fails then tell the truth.

His face changes when he hears the word 'Desiree'. And it doesn't change for the better. The lines in his forehead deepen, his mouth gets smaller and meaner and the veins in his neck start to bulge. Unfortunately his face isn't the only thing to register a reaction. His arm does too. It shoots out and grabs me by the neck and pulls.

My body has got two options here. One is to

abandon my neck to a solo career and leave the rest of my body to try and work without it. But, like so many pop bands, I'm sure that once one bit of it's gone it won't to be too long before the rest falls apart. So, I take the other option and follow my neck. Together we are dragged through the door and into the hall. The man pushes the door behind us and throws me up against the wall.

I figure this is a time to be very frightened. My legs agree because they start shaking and however much I try they just won't stop.

'What do you want with Desiree?' he demands.

This guy is taking the over-protective father to extremes. Behind him the dog is going mad, jumping up and down and barking and growling. I keep my main focus on the man but while I'm doing that I still find time to notice that the dog is a pit bull terrier. One of those ugly white ones with a big head and snapping jaws. The type of dog that is on the local news twice a week because their favourite food appears to be babies.

'Are you with the press?' the man says.

'What?' I haven't a clue where that question came from.

'Get down, Gandhi,' the man yells at the dog.

The dog ignores him and starts jumping higher, barking louder and growling even more aggressively.

'What's all this noise?'

A door opens at the bottom of the hall and a woman pokes her head round.

'I think we got a reporter,' shouts the man. 'You remember they told us that they might be sniffing round.'

'What?' The woman comes into the hall. 'If it's a reporter let Gandhi have him.'

I'm terrified. My heart is doing about two thousand beats per minute. I definitely don't want to be dog food.

'I'm not a reporter!' I shout as loudly as I can.

'He says he's not a reporter,' the man tells the woman.

'I'm not deaf, am I?' the woman points out to the man.

'But he could be lying,' the man tells the woman.

'I'm not a reporter. I'm not a reporter. I'm not a reporter,' I repeat.

The woman comes up to my end of the hall and pushes past Gandhi. She gives me a long hard look then turns away.

'What have you done, you fool?' she says to the man.

'What? I haven't done anything. I...'

'Look at him.'

'I am looking at him. Who do you think I'm looking at?'

The two of them starting a row has a bad effect on the dog's mood. To add to its attractive jumping, barking and growling skills it's begun foaming at the mouth. Sooner or later it's going to get past the man and bite through my leg.

'How old do you think he is?'

'I don't know.'

'Fourteen,' I tell them helpfully.

'Fourteen,' repeats the woman. 'And fourteen year olds aren't reporters.'

'Aren't they?' says the man.

'No,' says the woman. 'You've grabbed an innocent boy.'

'Oh,' says the man, taking a step backwards. 'That's not good.'

What sounds even less good is the triumphant bark of Gandhi, the pit bull terrier. When the man steps back, he leaves a big enough gap for it to get past. It takes the opportunity and charges, jaws open, drool dripping out of its gaping mouth.

'Aaarrrggghhh,' I say. My memory picks this moment to remind me that when dogs foam at the mouth it means that they might have rabies.

I'm so scared that I can't move. Frozen against the wall I just wait to feel its teeth tearing into my flesh.

But they don't.

The dog is still jumping at me with its mouth wide open but it isn't getting any nearer. The man has grabbed the dog by its tail and is holding it back.

'Here, Gandhi!' he shouts. 'Good dog. Don't eat the

nice boy because then the police will come and Daddy will get heavily fined for not having you neutered.'

Of the four creatures in the hall, three of us are stuck in positions we are finding it hard to get out of. The dog seems entirely happy with his continued attempts to make me his dinner. The man is therefore tied to his role of trying to prevent that and I'm not prepared to change my part of backing into the wall because any attempt to move forward would put my legs in reach of those jaws.

Which leaves the woman.

Who opens the door and disappears into the kitchen.

She comes back with a big stick. She smacks Gandhi once on his side. Gandhi stops barking and starts whimpering. Normally, I'm against cruelty to animals but in this case I'm prepared to make an exception.

The man drags Gandhi through a door and shuts him away.

I breathe for the first time in two minutes.

'Hello,' says the woman, 'I'm Desiree's mother.'

'Hi,' says the man, 'I'm Desiree's father.'

'Sorry about Gandhi being a bit playful,' says Desiree's dad.

'Puppies, eh?' adds Desiree's mum. 'Always into mischief.'

Always into mischief. I can't believe this. It was

almost into my tendons after making a detour through my skin and muscle.

'You're probably wondering why he's called Gandhi,' says Desiree's dad.

That wasn't what I was wondering. What I was wondering was why people keep animals in their houses that can eat people. What's wrong with tropical fish? Or hamsters?

'I didn't want to call him Gandhi,' says Desiree's dad. 'I wanted to call him Tyson. But he wouldn't answer to Tyson no matter how much I tried. And then there was this documentary on the TV and it was all about Gandhi. Thin bloke. From India. And every time they said Gandhi on the TV the dog went over to the TV and licked it. And then when I said Gandhi, he came over and licked me. So I had to call him it even though it gets me no end of abuse at pit bull terrier shows. I'll never watch BBC2 again.'

I smile in what I hope is a friendly way. I've still got to get out of this hall alive and just because the dog has gone doesn't mean that I'm going to succeed.

' So, what did you want with Desiree?' he asks.

Something tells me that explaining that I'm a detective who has been employed to look for her because the members of her rap crew think she's disappeared is not the right answer to this question.

'Yes,' adds the woman, who seems to be getting

15

suspicious all over again 'What do you want with her?'

I look from one to the other. I can hear Gandhi barking and then scratching at the door. He obviously still hasn't given up on the idea of having me for dinner.

I try to think of everything that I know about Desiree to give me some kind of decent explanation about why I'm here to see her. She's a good singer. That's no help. She's dumb. That wouldn't explain why anybody would want to come and see her. She's pretty. That just might.

'Please don't get angry,' I say.

'Why should I get angry?' says Desiree's dad sounding like he's getting angry.

'But the truth is...'

'Yes,' says Desiree's mum.

'I wanted to ask her out.'

'What?' shouts Desiree's dad.

Gandhi starts banging against the door and howling.

'I mean I wouldn't do anything,' I explain desperately, 'Or try anything on that she didn't want to do.' That doesn't sound too good so I try and make it sound better. 'Actually, even if she wanted to do anything then I wouldn't because I respect her too much and you too much too. I'm a very respectful type of boy.'

And then I realise I don't need to explain any more

because they are both laughing so loudly that they can't hear me.

I don't have much option so I stand there waiting until they've stopped which eventually they do.

'That's great,' says Desiree's dad. 'I haven't laughed so much in ages.'

I can't resist asking,

'What's so funny?'

'You wanting to go out with Desiree,' says her dad.

'She's sixteen going on twenty five,' says her mum. 'We spend most of our time trying to keep her away from going out with boys ten years older than her. They come round here with their sharp suits and their Rolex watches showing off their sports cars.'

'And then you turn up on a bike,' says her dad.

And they both start laughing again.

'It's got eighteen gears,' I point out.

That just makes them laugh even more.

I should be happy that my answer appears to have got me out of trouble. But the fact that they are humiliating me is taking some of the pleasure out of my success. Still a good detective must make use of every opportunity that is presented to him even if it is at the cost of his own personal dignity.

'Could I still ask her?' I persist.

Tears are pouring down their cheeks.

'She might be getting bored of older men and want to spend some time with somebody nearer her own age.'

They're holding on to each other now.

'At least let me try,' I say. 'Is she here now?'

Desiree's mum shakes her head.

'Could you tell me where she is or when she'll be back?'

'You should go now,' says Desiree's mum. 'Believe me when I tell you that I'm saving you from a big let down.'

Desiree's dad opens the door.

I've got no option. I walk through it.

Behind me I hear can hear them laughing. The rain is lashing down even worse than it was before I was dragged in. I pick up my bike and get on it. I can still hear Gandhi howling as I ride down the drive.

CHAPTER 3

By the time I've cycled home I've managed to put the image of Desiree's parents laughing at me out of my mind. I leave my bike in the garage and head into the house. My mum and Karen, my sister, are in the front room watching TV. My dad isn't anywhere to be seen which is fine by me.

'Mickey,' says my mum. 'Where have you been?'

'Out,' I tell her. You should never give a parent more than the absolute minimum of information.

'Ugh,' says Karen. 'You're soaked. You're dripping everywhere.'

'Go upstairs and get yourself a hot shower and some clean clothes,' my mum says. 'Your tea's been in the oven for over an hour. It's probably spoilt by now.'

'What is it?'

'Chicken, chips and peas.'

'What?' I can't believe it. We almost never get chips because Karen goes on and on about how unhealthy they are and we never get chicken because Karen's

19

a vegetarian. And now I've missed one of the few times when my mum could be bothered to make two different meals. I can't believe it.

'Chicken,' I repeat. 'Really?'

Karen snorts.

'You're all murderers,' she points out. 'That chicken had done nothing to you and then you go and eat it. It's like a crime.'

'Can I have it now?' I ask.

'Not until you've had a shower and got changed,' my mum answers. 'I'm not having you catching your death of cold.'

'You see,' shouts Karen. 'You care about Mickey's death but you feel nothing at all for the poor chicken.'

I leave them to compare the relative merits of me and the chicken. It's a good thing my dad isn't in the room or I'd lose.

The prospect of chicken and chips gets me upstairs and into the shower in record time and once I've got the temperature right, I'm able to think about the case.

The first thing is to admit that I was wrong. Well, I wasn't wrong but my hunch was. Maybe it wasn't a hunch after all. Maybe it was a theory disguised as a hunch. Or even a guess. Whatever. It does look like something has happened to Desiree. She didn't appear to be in like I thought she was and then when

I mentioned her name her dad grabbed me and demanded to know if I was a reporter. That means one of two things. Either Desiree is involved in something that might make the news but they want to keep quiet or Desiree's dad is mad and is always dragging people into his hall. Sadly, I've got to rule the second possibility out.

This means that Desiree's involved in something that her parents know about but the Really Tough Crew don't. And it's something that might interest a reporter. All I know about Desiree is that she's a good singer, she's pretty, she's dumb and lots of rich older blokes fancy her.

She must have a story. You don't get to have a story just from being dumb or by being a good singer (unless you've had a big hit which she hasn't). You don't even get in the paper for just being pretty unless you take most of your clothes off and having met her dad I don't see him letting that happen. Which leaves a rich older man fancying her. There could be a story there. Maybe she's been asked out by a famous guy or a member of the Royal family and it turns out that they were married and so they were cheating on their wife with a girl who was only sixteen. That's the kind of story that would get the press excited. But maybe the rich guy found out the press were onto him and were looking for Desiree to see if it was true. And so he paid for Desiree to go off to hide somewhere like a posh hotel and gave her parents lots of money so that they won't tell anybody where she is. Then, when I knock on the door asking for Desiree, her dad gets it straight into his head that I'm a reporter and grabs me and threatens to feed me to the dog.

That must be it.

I'm so staggered with my own detecting abilities that I stop washing my hair in order to admire myself in the bathroom mirror. Pretty soon the police will be coming round to my shed just begging me to make sense of their clues for them. Unfortunately, I'm so busy thinking what a great job I'm doing that the shampoo gets in my eyes and stings like crazy. That's what's wrong with life. Just when you're really pleased with yourself you do something stupid that makes you realise you were an idiot all along. I chuck tons of cold water in my face but my eyes still take ages to stop stinging.

'What have you been doing?' demands my mum when I go back into the front room carrying my dinner on a tray.

'I got distracted when I was having a shower,' I explain.

'I don't even want to think about what distracted you in the shower,' says Karen.

I go and sit down on the couch.

'Don't bring that chicken near me,' orders Karen.

'It's organic,' my mum tells her.

Somehow I don't think that is going to make it any better.

'It's still dead, isn't it?' says Karen.

'Yes, but it's going to a good home,' I say taking a large bite.

'Mickey,' warns my mum.

'I hope you get salmonella,' says Karen.

'Karen,' warns my mum.

'What about your make-up?' I ask her. 'That's all tested on animals. I bet this chicken would rather have had a happy life running round the field with all its mates and then one chop with a big knife and it's dead and I'm eating it. I bet it would rather that than spend its whole life in a some laboratory somewhere covered in mascara.'

I smile at Karen and stick a big fat chip in my mouth. We've been doing animal rights in PSE with Ms Walter.

'For your information,' says Karen. 'All my make-up is ethical. I only buy stuff from shops where they don't do any animal testing at all.'

'Oh.' I didn't know that. I can't think of anything to say now. I switch my attention to the TV to make it seem like I don't care. There's a detective thing starting which I want to watch.

Karen reaches for the remote but my reflexes are fast and I grab it fast. The person with the remote is the person with power.

'Mum, I want to watch The Hits Show,' whines Karen.

'I want to watch this,' I say.

'This is boring.'

'You chose what to watch last.'

'You were out.'

'You still chose.'

'Mum!'

Every other family in the world apart from ours has at least two TVs which prevents this kind of argument. All of my friends have got TVs in their rooms. We used to have two but one of them broke and because my dad lost his job he says we can't have a new one. I don't know what not having a job has to do with it. Most of the kids in my class whose mum and dad haven't got jobs haven't just got a TV each. They've got cable too.

'I suppose as this is on then we should leave it,' says my mum.

Victory. Karen admits defeat by grabbing the remote and switching on record on the video – my dad still won't get a DVD. I settle down to watch the detective show. Sometimes there's a crucial clue really early on and if you miss that then you haven't got a chance of being able to solve it.

The door opens and my dad comes in.

'How was your mother?' says my mum.

'She was fine,' says my dad, 'but disappointed not to see her grandchildren.'

Neither me or Karen look at my dad. He's always going on about how we should go and see our gran more.

'It's a shame,' he carries on, 'That in her twilight years, her eyesight failing, stuck in sheltered accommodation she is denied one of the few pleasures still left to her.'

The few pleasures left to her! He's really laying it on thick. My gran has loads of pleasures left to her. She's not stuck in sheltered accommodation. She's got one of those things like a little golf buggy and she drives it all over town banging into people deliberately. She loves going shopping because she can tell the people in the shops that they're robbing her of her pension because they charge more than they did in 1965. And if her eyesight is failing how come she can spot a microscopic bit of dinner stuck on my jumper like she did last time I went over and use it as an excuse to give me a lecture on personal hygiene and table manners?

'What's this?' says my dad looking at the TV. There's something about his tone that I don't like.

'It's that detective thing,' my mum tells him. 'Mickey's watching it.'

'Oh no, we can't have that,' my dad shakes his head and walks over to the TV.

'What?' I say. 'I've watched it loads of times.'

'Yes,' says my dad standing right in front of the TV to make sure that I can't see it. 'But now things are different.'

'What things?' I demand.

'What do you notice about the TV?'

There's nothing to notice about the TV. It's the same as it always is.

'Dad, can you move out of the way, please. I'm missing the autopsy.'

My dad ignores me and pulls a box out from behind the TV that I hadn't noticed before. It's got a wire running into the back of the set.

'What do you think this box means?'

'Cable!'

Me and Karen say exactly the same thing at the same time. If my dad has changed his mind and got cable then I'm prepared to miss my detective show for it.

'Don't be stupid.' He shakes his head angrily. 'Haven't I always said that five channels is more than enough?'

Nobody answers.

'No,' he carries on. 'This box which was installed today in carefully selected homes is provided free of charge by BARB. They're the people who monitor what shows a sample of the British people watch and from that they work out what ratings each programme has.'

He stops and waits for a reaction.

'That's nice,' my mum says eventually.

'But this new privilege brings responsibilities. We can affect the viewing habits of the whole of the nation.

If we watch a show then the programme makers will think that's the type of programme that people want to see and then they will make more of them. So we must only watch good television programmes.'

I don't like the sound of this.

'From now on we will only watch nature programmes, documentaries and the news.'

My mum, Karen and me all shout at him at the same time. My mum loves anything with doctors in it like Casualty or ER. Karen is addicted to this programme about being a model on Channel 4 and I like detective stuff. All of them seem to be banned. The only person who won't mind is my dad. Guess what he likes – nature programmes, documentaries and the news.

My dad holds up his hand for silence. He seems to be enjoying this.

'However,' he says, 'I am willing to compromise.'

Compromise is a word I didn't think my father knew.

'I have decided that when there are no nature programmes or documentaries or news on then and only then will we be able to watch the programme which is the most improving.'

'What do you mean by "improving"?' asks Karen. I can tell from her voice that she doesn't think 'improving' is the word that my dad would use to describe eight wannabe models living in some posh London flat and getting drunk all the time.

'Well let's take now as an example,' says my dad, picking up the Radio Times. 'On BBC1 we've got The Hits Show, on BBC2 we've got Celebrity Ready Steady Cook in the Garden, on ITV there's Holidays from Hell Part 8, on Channel 4 is Mickey's detective nonsense and on Channel 5, there's Baring it All, an in-depth documentary,' he pauses and then reads it again for emphasis. 'An in-depth documentary charting the rise of two girls in their quest to appear on Page 3 of... Well I don't know about that...'

His voice trails off.

'Do we have to watch Channel 5 then?' Karen asks. 'It's the only one with a documentary on.'

'We're not watching that,' snaps my dad. 'That's not a proper documentary. Documentaries are about poor people or science. No, it's obvious that Channel 5 is too crude and exploitative, ITV is for idiots, BBC2's out because there are too many cooking shows and Channel 4's not on because there are too many detective shows. Which leaves...The Hits Show. That's what we should watch. A show that is about an art form. Even if it is a somewhat debased art form.'

My dad walks over to the remote control and flicks the channel over to BBC1.

'That's not fair,' I say. 'I was watching that. Mum said.'

'Your mother wasn't aware of all the facts,' says my dad. 'She didn't realise that we are no longer watching for ourselves. We are watching for our country.'

'Yeah, Mickey,' says Karen, who suddenly seems to think that Dad's new rules are fine as long as they mean that she gets to watch what she wants. 'Why don't you show a bit of patriotism for a change?'

I know I'm beaten. There's nothing to do but shut up and watch the TV.

This thrash metal band are just finishing off a song. You can tell that it's nearly finished because the lead singer's voice sounds like he's screaming in agony because a hamster is chewing through his vocal chords. The guitarist is just a demented tattoo with facial hair and the drummer looks like some early ancestor of human beings that we did in History in Year 7.

'These guys rock,' says Karen.

The lead singer does a massive leap in the air, the drummer does a roll and the guitarist smashes out the final chords. The crowd go crazy. I've never understood the crowd at The Hits Show. One minute they're all headbanging like mad when the Thrash Metal band are on and the next minute they're waving candles in the air while some ex-boy band member sings a song so slushy and sloppy that you feel like you're getting wet just watching it. It doesn't make sense.

'Hey y'all,' says the presenter.

'Look how thin she is,' says Karen.

'That was Decay by Zenith. Check out their album Putrification if you want to hear more tracks like that one. And now an all girl band that have shot straight in at number 9. With their first ever TV performance, let's hear it for Girl Power.'

You just need to hear the name to know what's coming. It's another all-girl group. One's blonde, one's black, one's dark, one's Asian and one's weird. They probably met each other for the first time last week and they all keep trying to shove each other out of the way whenever the camera goes near them so as to get their face on the TV as much as they can. They pretend that it's part of the dance routine but you can see that it isn't. The song is just the same as every girl group song that's ever been put out. There's some boy and they want him to be theirs but he's got to treat them right and hang out with their friends and then they'll be together forever and ever. After two choruses the one who is supposed to be weird does a rap to show that they aren't really just another girl group but instead they are real and street and hard. But you can tell so easily that she hasn't ever done a rap before. She looks really happy when it's over and she can get back to singing the soppy chorus with all the others. Finally the camera pans back from them so that you know it's over.

'Yo people that was happening,' yells the presenter. 'Give it up for Girl Power. We're going to be hearing loads more from them in the future but if you want to check them out live then they're playing Birmingham, Hanford, Liverpool and Manchester next week.'

'Who'd want to see them?' demands Karen.

For once I agree with her.

'And now,' says the presenter, 'This next band have flown over specially from the States to be here with us tonight. With their latest single from their platinum selling album 'Poisonous Despair' lets make some noise for...'

The Hits Show disappears from the screen. In its place is a nature programme. It's title comes up on the screen: 'The three-toed South American sloth.'

'Dad,' wails Karen. 'I was watching The Hits Show.'

'I said that we would only watch other programmes until a nature programme or an improving documentary came on. Well, now there's a nature programme on it takes priority.'

The camera zooms in on the sloth. It's asleep.

'But Dad,' whines Karen. 'This is rubbish.'

I agree with Karen twice within a minute. Sloths aren't the kind of animals that you should make nature programmes about. They should only make nature programmes about lions and crocodiles. Things that chase other things and then eat them. The rest of nature is just boring.

My dad ignores Karen. On the TV the sloth wakes up, yawns and then goes back to sleep again.

It's going to be a long night.

CHAPTER 4

'Mickey Sharp: failed.'

I knew I'd failed but I was hoping that Newman wouldn't notice. Newman's my form teacher. I thought he'd be all right when he started but with every week that goes by he gets more and more like all the other teachers. And in my school becoming more and more like other teachers is definitely a bad thing.

'Mickey, can you explain your failure?'

I look up at Newman. I can't explain my failure. He knows I can't explain my failure. I know he knows that I can't explain my failure. But still we're going to have to go through the motions.

I shrug.

'Don't shrug,' he says.

What I am not able to explain is my failure to meet my weekly target of credits. It's this new system that Mr Strangeways, the new deputy head started. Every week your form teacher looks at how many credits you got the week before. Then he decides how many credits you should get the next week. So, if you got ten last week he might decide that you should get fifteen. If you get them you've succeeded and if you don't then you've failed. If you succeed you get put in a raffle to win a book token which is the kind of prize that he probably thinks is going to get the whole school excited.

'Come on, Mickey,' Newman says. 'I want to know why you have failed to reach your target and I am prepared to wait for an answer.'

'I was unlucky,' I suggest.

'Try harder, Mickey.'

'It was discrimination.'

'Discrimination?' He arches an eyebrow.

'Yeah. All my teachers discriminate against me by not giving me credits because I'm late for class or because I forget my homework.'

Newman gives me his sarcastic smile.

'Mickey. What was your credit target this week?'

'Two.'

'And how many credits did you actually achieve?'

'None.'

'What does that tell you Mickey?'

'That I was close.'

'No, Mickey, it doesn't but I'll tell you what. Next week we'll make your target so easy to get that even you can't miss it. Your target is to get just one credit. What do you think of that?'

'It'll be a challenge.'

'Watch your step, Mickey. I stopped finding you funny months ago.'

He writes my target into next week's credit chart. 'Who's next?' He looks down at his list and reads out, 'Robert Foster. Passed. Well done, Robert.'

That's just typical. Robert Foster is one of the morons at the back. The morons at the back spend almost every lesson sticking compasses in each other's hands or hitting each other round the head with rulers or finding some other way to make each other bleed. They cause all our teachers loads of grief. I don't. I just sit there not listening. But they get more credits than me because the teacher wants to blackmail them into being quiet. All they need to do is shut up for five minutes. Newman knows that the number of credits means nothing because he used to make jokes about them when he first came. But now he's just like all the other teachers.

'Right. I think that's everybody,' Newman says. 'I just need to go next door to check I've got these targets right.'

He gets up from his desk and heads for the door.

'Remember the chart, sir,' shouts Katie Pierce.

The whole class laughs. Even me. Which is unusual when Katie Pierce is saying something because she's my biggest enemy.

'Oh yes.' Newman goes red and comes back to pick up his chart. 'Thank you, Katie.'

He rushes for the door before anybody can say anything else. He's still trying to con himself that we haven't noticed even though we all have. Even the Thick Girl with Glasses and the Even Thicker Girl with Pigtails have. What we've noticed is that he fancies Ms Walter. He's been coming up with stupid excuses to go round to her classroom for the last three weeks. Either he needs to borrow a board marker or he isn't sure exactly what the bulletin means or he's forgotten the maximum length of earrings that the girls are allowed to wear. If he wasn't a teacher you'd feel sorry for him. He hasn't got a chance with Ms Walter. I've got her for PSE and she's always talking about how women are beating men at everything now and that soon they're going to run the world. She says men have been running the world for centuries and they've made a big mess of it so it's about time that women were given a go because men are so clueless. And you look at Newman and he's exactly the type of useless man that she's talking about.

'What did you do last night?' says Umair suddenly.

Umair sits next to me so you'd think I wouldn't be surprised by him talking but I am. He used to be my best mate but we've kind of stopped this year after some teachers told his parents that I was a bad influence who was going to stop him getting anywhere in life. Registration is the only time that we still sit together these days and even then we hardly talk. And if we do, because we aren't friends like we used to be, I'd normally answer a question about what I did last night by saying something like 'Watched telly' but I can't resist telling him the truth this time because I've got such a good answer.

'I got dragged into a house by a mad bloke and nearly eaten by his dog,' I tell him.

'I had a boring evening as well,' says Umair.

He catches me for a second. I'm so not used to us talking to each other like friends that I'm on the edge of making a fool of myself by getting sarcastic and saying something about his visits to chess club. But I catch myself just in time and look at him. He's trying not to give anything away so neither am I.

'And then,' I add, 'just as this dog was about to eat me a flying saucer smashed through the roof of the house, a door opened at the bottom of it and I was sucked up into its central chamber and transported to a far off galaxy where alien life forms performed unpleasant experiments on me.'

Umair shakes his head.

'Those aliens,' he says. 'They've been causing no end of trouble down our way too.'

I crack first and start laughing. I can't help it. He's always been better than me at winding people up. I always exaggerate too much. He just plays it cool. But once I start laughing, he does too.

And so I tell him all about the case and what happened last night and how I've got to find Desiree before Saturday. I've never told him about a case before because I only started being a detective after we stopped being friends. I give him the full lowdown including my theory that Desiree's got involved with some celebrity or a member of the Royal family.

'Right,' nods Umair when I've finished. 'So how are you going to find out which celebrity or member of the Royal family it is?'

'Hello, boys.'

We were so busy chatting that neither of us noticed Katie Pierce come up to our desk.

'Hello Katie,' I say with a false smile.

'What are you chatting about?' she asks.

'Nothing.' Katie Pierce has been on the wrong end of some of the cases that I've solved in the past and it's got her into trouble. She's the last person that I'd tell about anything that was happening in my life.

'Oh, I understand,' Katie nods. 'You were talking about me. Most boys do.'

'Oh yeah?' I say trying to sound as sarcastic as possible.

'Yes,' she fakes a yawn. 'It's tiresome. But what can a girl do when she's a fantasy figure to an entire school.'

Her eyes flick to Umair.

'Is that hair on your top lip or have you just sneezed?' she demands.

Umair gets all embarrassed and looks away which is strange because he never used to be fazed by Katie. Maybe all that time he's spent at chess club has left him unable to cope with girls.

'I always say that when a boy is ready for a razor he's ready for me,' says Katie. Umair puts his head in his bag as though he's looking for something. I'm a bit disappointed. You should never ever let Katie Pierce embarrass you whatever she says because she'll go on doing it forever.

'I'll put you on my list,' says Katie to Umair. Or at least to Umair's back because the rest of him has vanished.

'What list?' I ask.

'You can't be on it, Mickey.'

'I didn't say that I...'

'I have it on good authority that you haven't hit puberty yet.'

'What are you talking about?'

'Let's just say that I've got my sources.'

Just in time I realise she's tricking me into asking a whole load of questions about myself which will give her the chance to insult me. But I'm not as dumb as I used to be. I pull out just in time and get back to the original question.

'What list?'

'My list of emergency boyfriends.'

'Why would you need a list of emergency boyfriends?'

'In case I finish with all three that I'm going out with at the moment and I need some eye candy on my arm. A girl needs a fall back position, Mickey.'

She suddenly fixes her eyes on me. She's got these big deep dark blue eyes and when she stops blinking and gives you the full treatment you feel like you can't look away. For a moment I'm caught by it. Me – who's seen loads of sad boys get trapped by her stare on full power can still suddenly find myself thinking that she's looking straight through my body and into my heart. But you can't let yourself be fooled. Otherwise you are just like a doomed mouse hypnotised by a king cobra. I tear my eyes away from hers but I can see from the sly smile that she knew she had me for a second.

'How many boys have you got on your list?' I ask to distract her.

'That's a good question, Mickey,' she answers. 'I'm always adding boys to it when they start to get good looking and then taking them off when they start to get acne. I think maybe I'll review my whole list at break time behind the sports hall while I'm having my mid-morning fag. But don't be disappointed that you're not on it. I'll consider you for a position when you get your first facial hair. In about ten years.'

I give her a sarcastic smile.

'Oh and Mickey,' she says, suddenly bending her head close to mine. 'Don't think that I haven't forgotten the trouble you've caused me recently. My mum is still carrying out random sniff tests on my breath to check for cigarettes and it's costing me a fortune in Polos.'

I got Katie caught smoking by her mum who comes into school to give the anti-smoking speeches.

'You could give up,' I suggest.

'When I want lifestyle advice from you, Mickey, I'll ask for it.'

'Whatever you say.'

'I've been busy recently, Mickey, but now I've got some time.'

'That's nice.'

'Do you know what I'm going to use this time for, Mickey?'

'Visiting senior citizens?' I suggest.

She shakes her head.

'Charity work?' I try.

'No, Mickey. I'm going to use this time for...' she leans in very close now so that her nose is almost touching mine.

'Revenge,' her final word comes out with a hiss. Then without waiting for a reply she pulls away and walks back to her desk.

The pips sounds for the end of registration.

I don't like to admit it but I'm nervous.

CHAPTER 5

Double Maths. Break. Double English. Single IT. Single Music. Lunch. Double Science.

They all go by and I'm riding home trying to work out what I've learnt during the day. The lessons have sort of merged into one so all I can remember is that the square of the hypotenuse equals an apostrophe plus a database minus a treble clef and that the result will react with water by fizzing briefly with a powerful purple flame. Or something like that.

When I'm halfway home it starts raining really hard. Every day I don't bring a coat to school it rains and every day I do it doesn't and I end up having to drag it round all day because all the lockers got vandalised last year. I try to ride faster but the faster I ride, the harder it rains. Within a couple of minutes it's turned into the sort of rain that hits the road and bounces back up off it and splashes you in the face. There are puddles everywhere and rain is running down the road like a mini-river. Some car goes past me way too close and sends up a big spray which covers my trousers and guarantees that my mum will give me a load of grief this evening.

Finally, I get back home, dump my bike in the garage and head straight to my shed. I need a swig of coke and a packet of salt'n'vinegar.

I pull open the door. And then I stop.

There's someone sitting in my chair, drinking my coke and eating my crisps.

And it's not Goldilocks.

'Yo!' says the crisp-and-coke stealer.

My shed is never the brightest place in the world but with the rain pounding down and black clouds all over the sky it's murkier than normal. I can see that there's a figure in my chair with some sort of hood on but that's about it.

'Yo!' says the voice again. 'You the man? You Mickey Sharp?'

I decide not to answer until I've got a better idea about who this kid is. I walk slowly and carefully over to the desk. I don't want to annoy this kid. If he's hard enough to walk into my shed and steal my coke'n'crisps then he might well be hard enough to give me a beating. The rain smashes even harder on the roof and behind it there's a distant rumble of thunder.

I get to my desk. The kid leans forward in the chair. I can see him properly. I can't believe it. He's only about eleven.

'Know what is wrong with these crisps, man?'

I can't believe his front.

'I'll take that as a "no",' he says. 'What's wrong with these crisps is that they is last year's brand. Nobody eats these anymore. Last year they were okay, the year before that they were hot but this year they are completely out. You need to pick out something else from the shelf next time.'

The arrogance of this kid. He's sitting in my shed, he's stolen my crisps and now he's insulting them.

'By the way,' he adds. 'Would you mind backing off a bit? You're dripping on me.'

I should hit him. I know I should. When you're fourteen and an eleven-year-old kid really asks for it you've got to hit him. Even if you don't want to. It's just the way the world works.

But I'm not much of a fan of hitting kids. I'm not much of a fan of hitting anybody really. I mean I've had fights. But I've never liked them. They're never as good as they look in films and even if you win your hands hurt afterwards. So, as there's nobody else here, I figure that I can take a chance and not hit the kid and nobody will ever know. The trouble is that I still have to find a way to show him that I'm not soft and that he can't be just walking into my shed and eating my crisps.

'You're probably wondering who I am?' he says.

'Tell me,' I say. I try and make it sound like an order.

'I'm Smarty,' he says.

'What?'

'It's my rapping alias,' he explains.

Another rapper. This must have something to do with the case.

'What do you want?' I say.

'You know my sister, Jenni,' he answers.

I look at him closely. He's definitely white. Jenni definitely isn't. They can't be brother and sister.

'You do know my sister, don't you?' he repeats.

I've got a case going on here and I'm not going to talk to some fake brother. This is no time to worry about people's feelings.

'I know a girl called Jenni,' I tell him. 'But I can't see how she can be your sister.'

'What d'you mean?' he demands.

'You're white and she's not.'

'We got different dads and the same mum.'

'Oh,' I say. That explains it.

'She's got business to do so she asked me to come over here and give you this photo of Desiree.' He stands up and pulls the photo out of his back pocket.

I put out my hand but he doesn't hand it over.

'But I'm telling you for nothing,' he says, 'That you're wasting your time looking for her.'

'Why?'

'I heard on the street what happened to her.'

'What?'

44

'She was caught in a drive-by. There's a turf war going on. Don't you know nothing?'

I can't believe what he's saying.

'You think she was shot?'

He shrugs.

'She comes from a tough neighbourhood.'

I know Hanford isn't exactly the nicest place in England but up to now I hadn't heard of too many drive-by shootings. But then again I was almost eaten by a pit bull terrier last night. So maybe...

And then I stop before I get carried away.

'Where's the body?' I ask.

'What?' he says.

'If someone's the victim of a drive-by shooting then there's going to be a body, isn't there?'

'Maybe.'

'Maybe?'

He looks at the ground. Then he shakes his head. Then he pulls his hood right up so I can hardly see him any more.

'Do you want the photo or not?' he says finally, thrusting out his hand.

I'm not letting him off that easy. Who does he think he is? Some eleven-year-old kid walking into my shed, sitting in my seat, drinking my coke, eating my crisps and telling me how to solve my cases.

'So you don't think it's a drive-by shooting now?' I ask.

'I don't know, do I?' he shrugs. 'You're the detective.'

'You're damn right I'm the detective,' I tell him.

I really like saying that. It makes me feel a lot better. I reach over and snap the photo out of his hands. I look at it once. I look at it twice. I look at it three times. And then I wait because this moment is going to be sweet.

'When you next see Jenni,' I tell him. 'You ask her to get over here.'

'Why?' he says.

'Because I've just solved the case.'

And however cool he's trying to be he can't stop his mouth from dropping open in amazement.

'But how?' he asks.

'Experience, kid,' I tell him. 'You can't buy it.'

CHAPTER 6

'Why don't you phone her and tell her yourself?' he says ten seconds later when he's remembered to shut his mouth.

This isn't what I wanted him to say. I wanted him to ask me what the solution to the case was because then I could tell him that I couldn't discuss that sort of confidential information with anybody except a client and look even cooler.

Instead he's hit me right on my weak spot. There's no reason why I shouldn't ring Jenni to let her know what's happened except that I don't have a mobile. It's pathetic. I'm the only person in our class who hasn't got one. I've tried everything to get one off my parents but they keep saying no. My sister has got one. They gave it to her in case of emergencies. I said what about me getting stuck in emergencies? My mum said I was a boy so it wasn't the same and my dad said I caused all the emergencies that he ever heard about. And then he started talking about how telephone boxes should all still be red so I gave up.

But I can't admit I haven't got a mobile to an eleven year old.

'My battery's flat,' I tell him.

'Guess, I'll have to use mine,' he says.

He reaches into his pocket and pulls out his mobile. It's small and slick and new. He makes sure I get a good eyeful of it.

'Take it outside,' I tell him. 'I need to think in here.'

Finally he gets out of my chair and heads for the door. I grab my chair back as soon as he's gone. I can hear him talking outside. Primary school kids with the latest phones and me with nothing. It's not right. The government or somebody should do something about it.

The door reopens and he's back inside fast.

'It's wet out there,' he says.

'If I want a weather forecast I'll switch on the TV,' I snap. His phone has really got to me.

'She's coming over now,' he says. 'She'll be here in five minutes.'

Seeing that I've got control of the chair back, he goes and sits on the box.

'What are you doing?'

'She told me to stay here and wait for her,' he says.

He doesn't even ask if it's okay to wait in the shed. If it wasn't for the fact that I'd be sounding like my gran I'd start saying that people don't have any manners any more.

Suddenly the shed feels too silent. It's strange how you hardly ever notice that it's quiet when you're on your own but as soon as there's somebody else in the room the silence is so loud that you can't miss it. That doesn't exactly make sense but I know what I mean.

After a minute Smarty starts banging on the box. Not like he's trying to smash it but like it's a drum.

DA DUM. DA DUM. DA DUM. DA DUM.

Because it's hollow it doesn't make a bad sound and with the rain crashing down in the background it sounds pretty menacing.

TCH TCH, DA DUM. TCH TCH, DA DUM.

I didn't mean to but after a minute I find myself joining in by walloping on my desk. It gives out a flatter sound than the box.

BAM, TCH TCH, DA DUM. BAM, TCH TCH, DA DUM. BAM, TCH,TCH. DA DUM.

Then he throws in a clap.

BAM, TCH TCH, DA DUM, CLAP. BAM, TCH TCH, DA DUM, CLAP. BAM, TCH,TCH, DA DUM, CLAP.

Then without any warning at all he starts rapping.

> *'Hey listen up, it's DJ Smarty*
> *Stuck in this stinking shed*
> *If I had a working Ouzi*
> *Everyone would be dead.'*

I'm straight out the hood
Now I'm in your place
Gonna take a sledgehammer
Smash it in your face.

I am from the Hanford posse
Be scared. Get ready to run
In the ghetto where I live
The only law is a gun.

He stops suddenly.

'That's how it is,' he says. 'Where I come from things are so tough that I don't even know if I'm gonna make it to be a teenager. Every night could be your last.'

'Where do you live?'

He looks uncomfortable.

'I live around,' he says.

'Around where?'

'In a block of flats,' he says which isn't answering my question.

'Where?'

'Hanford-on-the-Hill,' he mutters.

'Hanford-on-the-Hill,' I repeat an awful lot louder.

'Yeah,' he says. 'So what?'

It doesn't matter how hard he tries to make himself look, he isn't going to make me believe that Hanford-on-the-Hill is some tough ghetto. It's one of the poshest areas around. Any flats up there have got the word 'luxury' written in front of them first.

'There are some tough bits of the Hill,' he insists.

'Whatever you say,' I tell him.

He doesn't speak for a second but you can tell just by looking at him that he's got more to say. It doesn't take too long coming.

'It's not my fault that my mum is a solicitor,' he tells me. 'I told her that if I was going to become a proper rapper then we were going to have to go and live in a trailer park but she wouldn't listen. She said the best she could manage was a caravan holiday in Wales.'

The door opens which saves me from having to listen to little rich boy tell me how terrible it is not to have nothing.

It's Jenni.

'This better be good,' she says.

'It is,' I tell her.

'Let's hear it then.'

Never rush moments like these. Moments where you are going to look really cool because believe me they don't happen that often. I take a few seconds to check her out. She looks really good. She's got this baseball cap on the wrong way round and her dark hair is falling out of it. She's wearing a black Adidas jacket and jeans and cool white trainers. She's got one hand on her hip and a look that says 'impress me'. I plan to do my best.

'Come on,' she repeats. 'I got places to be.'

'I've solved your case,' I tell her.

She loses her cool for half a second when I say that. It's back almost before it's missing but I spot it. I'm not a detective for nothing. It makes me feel good to know that I can impress her.

'So,' she says. 'Where is she?'

'I don't know where she is now,' I tell her, 'but I can tell you where she was at 7.30 last night.'

'Is that what I asked?' she shoots back.

'It's what you're getting,' I tell her. When you've got a piece of information as big as this you feel like you can act just as tough back.

She looks at me. Smarty looks at me. I've dragged this out as long as I can.

'She was on The Hits Show.'

'What?' they both say at the same time.

'She was the black girl in Girl Power. They're new at number nine in the charts.'

Neither of them say anything for a second.

'The cow.'

Then Jenni does.

'The lying two-faced cow.'

She keeps going.

'The lying, two-faced, back-stabbing, deceitful cow.'

Once she starts there isn't any stopping her.

'The lying, two-faced, back-stabbing, deceitful, selfish, vain...'

'Hey,' I interrupt. 'Could you show off your knowledge of nouns some other time.'

She transfers all the anger and contempt that she's been aiming at Desiree onto me.

'They're not nouns, they're adjectives.'

'Oh.' I knew I should have listened more in English. 'Anyway, the point is I've solved the case. I've found Desiree. That will be ten pounds, please.'

Her face changes from anger and contempt to rage.

'What d'you mean?' she shouts. 'The deal was that you found her and got her to come to the record company demo session. I don't see her here so I don't see how you've solved the case.'

Now it's my turn to get angry.

'That was before we knew where she was,' I tell her. 'Now we know she's in a group with a hit we know that she isn't going to come to your recording session. It's obvious. She's left the Crew on purpose. That's why she's been ignoring your calls and why she's going to keep on ignoring them. She's already in the charts and on The Hits Show. I nearly got eaten by her dog because her mum and dad were keeping it a big secret and thought I was a journalist. This is her big shot at fame. She isn't going to suddenly decide that she's going to give it all up to go back with a group who haven't even got a record deal.'

'That's not my problem,' she says. 'That's yours. You took the case. Nobody forced you.'

'Hey!' I say. 'Let's be sensible here. You know and I

know that she's left your crew for another band. She's made her decision. Nobody is going to change it.'

'Well, you're gonna have to,' she slams back. 'I've got three witnesses who heard you say that you'd take the case and get her back for the recording session. You're the kind of guy that talks big but don't deliver.'

'No, I'm not,' I say. 'I'm just recognising that the situation is different.'

'You can't hit the ball,' she tells me. 'You shouldn't step up to the plate.'

'Jenni,' I protest. 'Let's be reasonable here.'

'No way,' she says. 'You took a contract. You got to fulfil it.'

'But I can't.'

'You mean you won't.'

'I know what I mean and I mean I can't.'

'You haven't even tried.'

'But she's already a pop star.'

'So?'

I stop for a second. Why can't this girl see what is really obvious to me? Desiree isn't coming back.

'Let me tell you something,' Jenni says. 'I don't like being let down. And if you don't solve this case do you know what I'm going to do?'

'No.'

'When I do get a record deal I'm going to make sure that my first single, which will be a massive seller worldwide, is called '*Mickey Sharp Lets You Down.*'

'What?' I say.

'I can feel the words coming to me already,' she says. 'It's going to be one phat track.'

'But you can't.'

'Hit that box,' she says turning to DJ Smarty.

BAM BAM TIC TIC BAM BAM

Straightaway he's got a beat going.

'Hold on,' I say but she isn't listening any more. Her eyes are shut and her head is nodding to the rhythm. Smarty keeps hitting the box. Her eyes flash open and she starts.

'Brothers and sisters listen up to me.
Gonna tell you 'bout a mother who's well shady.
Says he's a detective but he don't do enough
Bails on his clients when the going gets tough.

Likes to talk the talk sitting in his shed
But on the street he's nothing that's what I said.
He says he'll help but I know he's bluffing
Promises you everything gives you nothing.

So going out to all the sisters in this town
Don't trust Mickey Sharp, he lets you down.
Pretends he's a man but he's nothing but a clown.
Don't trust Mickey Sharp, he lets you down.
Yeah
Don't trust Mickey Sharp he lets you down

The beat stops. She stares at me.

'If you don't get back on the case then I'm putting out that rap at every gig I ever do. So even if I don't get a record deal then your rep will still be ruined in Hanford. Understand?'

This is terrible. A detective lives and dies by his reputation. If the coolest crew in Hanford start rapping about not trusting me then I could end up with no cases at all.

'I understand,' I tell her.

'Good,' she says. 'And just to make sure you aren't just saying it I want my brother here to be your assistant on the rest of the case so that if you stop working then I'll know about it.'

'I work alone,' I tell her firmly.

'*Don't trust Mickey Sharp, he lets you down,*' she repeats.

'But I've always been prepared to compromise,' I tell her weakly.

'Good.'

I look at DJ Smarty.

'Meet me back here tomorrow after school.'

'OK,' he says. 'If I live through the night.'

He walks out. Jenni follows him. The shed door bangs shut behind them.

I stare at it for a while. Then I pull open a drawer and grab a coke and a bag of salt'n'vinegar and start munching and slurping. I try to think of any idea, no matter how mad, that might make someone leave a successful pop group to join an unsuccessful rap crew. But my head stays a total blank. After a while I stop thinking about Desiree and start thinking about Jenni. There must be something wrong with me. She's just been totally unreasonable and put me in a position where I've got to do something which I haven't got a chance of pulling off. And instead of hating her all I can think of is that it would be good to see her again. There was something about the way she looked at me. Something else beside the anger and contempt. Or maybe it was the anger and the contempt. I don't know. Whatever it was it worked.

I realise that I'm humming. And then I stop because I realise what I'm humming. The tune to *Mickey Sharp, He'll Let You Down*. I really need to solve this case because I can't let that rap out into the world.

It's catchy.

CHAPTER 7

It came to me in a dream. I went to sleep without the faintest idea what to do and I woke up this morning with a brilliant solution. Sleep has helped me solve a problem. I wonder if I should suggest it to Mr Barlow to see if it helps us in Maths. What am I doing thinking about Maths when I've just come up with a great plan for solving the case? It's like this...

'Mickey get down here now. You're going to be late.'

'I know,' I shout. Every day my mum tells me I'm going to be late like I don't know. Does she think I can't tell the time?

'I want to see you dressed in your school uniform before I go to work.'

'There's a picture of me in my school uniform on the sideboard,' I shout back down. 'Why don't you look at that?'

It's not actually the right school uniform because it's a picture of me on my first day at primary school. My dad used to take pictures of me then.

'Don't make me come up those stairs and get you,' shouts my mum.

'I'm not making you do anything,' I shout back. 'You have free will. We did it in PSE.'

'I might have free will,' shouts back my mum, 'But you don't. You have my will which says get downstairs now and have your breakfast.'

There's nothing for it. I'm going to have to get out of bed. My school uniform is where I left it last night – on the floor. My mum is going through one of her 'it's your room you keep it the way you want' phases which normally lasts until the mess starts spilling out onto the landing. Then she says that she's going to come in to my room and everything that's on the floor is going to get thrown away. Every time she says that I make sure that my school uniform is lying on the floor and every time it gets picked up and put on a hanger. Parents only keep the threats they want to.

Anyway I get dressed fast and head downstairs. I'll come back up later to clean my teeth and stuff because it's still halfway into Karen's morning hour in the bathroom and you never hurry her up unless you're prepared for a long lecture on the importance of moisturiser on combination skin. And I'm still too woozy from sleep for that.

'You look a mess,' says my mum as soon as I walk into the kitchen.

'Thanks,' I tell her.

'Your hair needs sorting out, your shirt's not tucked in and your top button is undone.'

'How are my socks?' I say trying to find something that she can be positive about.

'I can't smell them from here,' she says, 'Which is a good sign. I've poured out your muesli.'

'Isn't there anything else?' I hate muesli. It's another of Karen's healthy ideas.

'No there isn't,' says my mum. 'And anyway muesli is good for you.'

'Not even any toast?'

'No. You should be glad of muesli.'

'Why?'

My mum looks confused.

'Lots of reasons,' she says. 'The Swiss eat it all the time.'

'So?' I say.

'They're a successful nation,' says my mum. 'They have alps and cowbells and overhanging roofs.'

I can tell she's on the run. She's not looking at me any more.

'That's rubbish,' I tell her. 'What else have the Swiss done?'

My mum goes over to the kitchen sink and starts doing the washing up.

'Mum?'

'Oh I don't know,' she says, slapping her scourer into a pot. 'The cuckoo clock.'

'The cuckoo clock,' I repeat. 'That's what muesli does for you. Look at the British. We invented football and gravity and the Spinning Jenny thanks to bacon and egg.'

My mum doesn't answer. She just keeps washing up.

'So, I think I should have bacon and egg,' I suggest. 'It will make me more likely to succeed.'

And it's loads nicer. And it will upset Karen.

'You're having muesli,' says my mother in one of those this-discussion-is-over voices.

There's nothing else to do. I pick up the milk and start to pour. It's the last bit of the packet which makes it worse. There isn't a nut or a raisin in sight, just white shavings of what look like bits of wood. I might as well go back to primary school and eat the stuff they put in the bottom of the hamster cage.

My dad walks in and grunts which is his way of saying 'Good morning.' Our science teacher in school was going on about how amazing human beings were because they were constantly evolving and improving and one of the most fantastic ways that we had succeeded was in the continued development and sophistication of our communication skills through language. He's obviously never seen my dad before he's had his first cup of coffee. It's like Neanderthal man has made a comeback.

'There's nothing but junk mail here,' says my dad flicking through the post. 'They should ban it.'

I keep my head down. Once my dad's found one thing to irritate him like junk mail then he's going to find something else quite soon. And that is likely to be me.

'What's this?'

I don't look up from my muesli.

'Who's writing to you then, Mickey?'

This time I change my mind and I do look up. My dad is holding a letter in his hand. It's got my name on.

Nobody ever writes to me. Except on birthdays and then it's only cards so they don't count. Some of the cards don't even have money in them so they count even less.

I rip open the envelope. There's a piece of paper inside. I pull it out. It says:

IF YOU WANT TO KNOW WHERE TO FIND DESIREE THEN BE AT THE WASTE GROUND BEHIND THE SEWAGE WORKS AT 4.15 THIS EVENING.

A FRIEND

'What is it?' says my dad.

'Nothing,' I tell him. My dad isn't the biggest fan of me being a detective so I tend to give it a low profile around him.

'It must be something,' insists my dad.

'Yeah,' I say.

'Well, what is it?'

'It's a letter.'

'Don't be cheeky. What does it say?'

That's the thing with my dad. He tells you that almost everything you do is worthless but he still wants to know all about it.

I take a deep breath.

'It's private,' I tell him.

'I don't think letters that come to my house should be seen as private from me,' my dad fires back.

'I do,' I say. It's risking one of his temper explosions to say this to him but I don't care. It is my letter and I've got a right to keep it to myself.

'So do I,' adds my mum.

'What?'

'Mickey's got a right to keep his correspondence private,' says my mum. 'He's fourteen now. We've got to trust him a bit.'

My mouth falls open when my mum says that. A few bits of muesli drop onto the table.

'Ha!' My dad does one of his laughs that aren't really laughs. 'What always happens when we trust Mickey. Within a week we're sitting in his headteacher's office begging for one more chance.'

'It's my address too and I think he's entitled to keep his letters to himself. It might be from a female admirer.'

I could have done without that line from my mum.

But her backing me up is so unusual that I'm prepared to live with it.

'A female serial killer more like knowing Mickey,' grumbles back my dad but he gives up trying to sneak a look at the letter. I get out of the kitchen before he changes his mind. But I make sure that I swallow the last of my sawdust flavoured muesli before I do. It's my way of saying thanks to my mum for helping me out.

CHAPTER 8

I get out of the house so fast I'm actually early setting off for school. And by the time I get there I'm even earlier because it's pouring down with rain again which means that I ride faster. But by the time I get there I'm soaked.

I lock up my bike and head into school.

'Where are you going?'

Just as I get inside the main entrance Mr Walton comes out of his office and spots me.

'I'm going to my tutor room.'

'You aren't allowed in yet. The first bell hasn't gone. Get back outside.'

A particularly big drop of rain runs down my nose and drops off the end like a lousy ski jumper. I decide to appeal to Walton's better nature.

'But it's pouring with rain and I'm soaked.'

'Rules are rules, Sharp. And my legal obligation to you in terms of 'in loco parentis' does not commence until the first bell goes. So get outside now.'

'But I might catch pneumonia and die.'

'Then you will go to your grave in the happy knowledge that you died while obeying the school rules. I may even award you a posthumous credit. Now get out.'

I've got no choice. I walk back out into the pouring rain.

That tells you everything you need to know about our school. If you listened at assembly you'd hear all this stuff about how 'the school is a community' and 'we are all in this together' and how 'only by working together will we succeed in ridding ourselves of the tarnished reputation falsely fostered by the last two OFSTED reports.' We always need to think about 'community' when it's time to pick up the litter. But nobody says 'community' much when the kids have to stand outside in the rain while the teachers sit in the staff room stuffing their faces with chocolate biscuits.

Not that I intend to stand outside in the rain. I head straight round to the back of the school, find an entrance that nobody's watching and head upstairs to my tutor room. There is a very warm radiator in there that is just waiting for me to come and lean on it.

There's already two people in there when I get in – the Thick Girl with Glasses and the Even Thicker Girl with Pigtails. They're standing on chairs at the back of the room facing the wall. Normally I wouldn't talk to them but they're doing something so stupid that I have to ask.

'What are you doing?'

They both turn round. Then they look at each other. Then they look at me. Then they look at each other again. Finally the Thick Girl with Glasses opens her mouth.

'Mr Newman said we could come in early and tidy up his display boards.'

'What?'

'Mr Newman said we could...'

'I heard. What I mean is just because he says you can come in and tidy up his display boards why are you doing it?'

'I knew I shouldn't have talked to you,' said the Thick Girl with Glasses. 'You'll try and spoil everything.'

'Let's ignore him,' says the Even Thicker Girl with Pigtails.

'Yes, let's,' says the Thick Girl with Glasses.

And they both turn their backs on me.

I'm used to attractive girls giving me the silent treatment but now I'm being snubbed by girls I didn't even want to talk to in the first place. I'm not sure whether that's a good sign or a bad sign so I decide it's bad to be on the safe side. Then I won't be disappointed.

I park myself tight against the radiator and let it do its work on my soaking school uniform. This is the first time today I've been able to think about my brilliant idea. And that's when I realise that it isn't there any more.

That's the problem with having a plan come to you in your sleep. It fades just as swiftly as a dream. I close my eyes and try to concentrate. I know that the plan is still somewhere in my head but I've got to find it. What was I thinking just before my mum shouted up to me that I had to get up. I was thinking about the...

'Ow!'

My eyes open.

'I've just stuck a drawing pin in my thumb.'

'You're bleeding on the display. We won't get any credits if we leave blood all over the homework timetable.'

'I'm going to get a tissue.'

'I'm coming with you.'

They both get off their chairs and head out of the room, making sure to keep ignoring me on their way.

Alone at last.

I close my eyes again and concentrate. I try to travel back in time to the moment when I woke up. I don't know how to travel back in time but I imagine it's like when you rewind a video but you can still see the picture on the screen. So I cycle home backwards and then I walk in through the door backwards and then I sit at the table and take muesli out of my mouth with a spoon and put it back into the bowl and then I go back upstairs take off my clothes and get into bed and then I close my eyes and...

Nothing.

No, maybe something.

False alarm. It was just a yawn.

I scrunch my eyes up really tightly and try and focus my entire brain on that moment when I woke up. When my mind was clear and the plan was bouncing around in my head like a perky red balloon.

Suddenly I've got it.

My plan was this: they said on The Hits Show that Girl Power were going to be playing a gig this week at the Hanford Colosseum. If I can get down there then I can mingle with the fans and when the time comes maybe I can talk to Desiree and explain to her that she's got to come back and join the Really Tough Crew just for one session.

I keep thinking but there doesn't seem to be any more. Standing here in the harsh neon strip light of my classroom the plan doesn't seem anywhere near as good as it did when I'd just woken up.

Still it's all I've got.

Isn't it?

No.

I've also got the letter. I pull it out of my pocket and smooth it out. Who can it be from? What could whoever wrote it have to tell me about Desiree? There's only one way to find out. I have to go.

The classroom door opens. In comes Katie Pierce. She stops and stares like she's really shocked to see me.

'Mickey,' she says. 'There's steam coming off you.'

'I got wet,' I tell her.

'Tell yourself that,' she says. 'But I know it's the sight of me that's got you all steamy. When are you going to learn Mickey – I'm out of your league?'

She gives me a pitying smile. Behind her, Umair comes through the door. He looks really surprised to see me too. Maybe I'm late for school more often than I thought. He doesn't look as surprised to see Katie even though I'm sure she's late way more times than I am.

Katie sits down gets out her mobile phone and starts phoning someone or texting them or something. Umair comes over and leans against the radiator next to me.

'JULIE, WHERE ARE YOU?' Katie Pierce shouts into her mobile phone. She's not exactly quiet most of the time but when she's on the phone she's twice as bad. 'I'M IN OUR CLASSROOM. ARE THERE ANY FIT BOYS NEAR YOU? THERE ARE? WHERE? STAY THERE. I'LL BE THERE IN TWO MINUTES. DON'T LET THEM OUT OF YOUR SIGHT.'

She grabs her bag and rushes out of the room. I feel sorry for whichever fit boys are about to be given Katie's undivided attention. It won't be long in our school before boys are having plastic surgery to make themselves uglier so that Katie Pierce doesn't get interested in them.

'How's your case going?' Umair asks as soon as she's out of the room.

I don't normally tell people about my cases partly because I say 'confidentiality guaranteed' on the advert but mainly because nobody is interested. But Umair doesn't know anybody in the world of rap so I tell him what's been going on and about all the grief I've been getting from everybody. Then I tell him about my plan. He seems really interested and I get this idea in my head.

'Maybe you could come along,' I say. 'Help me get a few minutes with Desiree.'

He stops looking interested when I say that and starts looking worried.

'I don't think it's my kind of thing' he says, 'And anyway I've got a big chess match tonight.'

I didn't think there was such a thing as a 'big' chess match.

'What's so good about chess?' I ask because I've never been able to work it out.

'I don't know,' Umair answers. 'It's like fighting someone else's mind.'

'Maybe I'd be good at it,' I tell him. 'I'm always fighting someone else's mind. If it's not some teacher's, it's my dad's.'

The pips go for registration. Umair shakes his head.

'Chess might not be your game, Mickey,' he says. 'Because you've always got to be at least one move ahead of the opposition.'

CHAPTER 9

As far as the case goes I can't do anything until after school. Which means that I'm free to just have a normal day in school. Which means I'm going to be bored. Unless I do something to make it interesting. Something unusual. Like trying to reach my credit target. That would get Newman off my back. And how difficult can getting one credit be?

I start trying straight after registration.

'Can I take the register back for you, sir?' I ask Newman politely.

'Why?'

'To save you the trouble,' I explain.

He laughs at me and walks off still carrying the register.

On the way to my first lesson I see Miss Burley at the bottom of the stairs with a big box of books. Miss Burley teaches Food Technology. She also smokes all the time so she's always wheezing. You can smell it on her clothes. If you say anything about the smell she says someone in her GCSE group burnt their tuna bake but nobody believes her.

'Can I help you carry your books upstairs for you, miss?' I ask.

'What?' she says suspiciously.

'Can I help you carry your books upstairs?'

'What for?'

'I thought it might help.'

She looks doubtful. Then she looks at the stairs.

'All right,' she says, 'But I'll be right behind you.'

She hands over the box. It's heavier than I thought.

'Come on then,' she says. 'I didn't give you those books to stand there looking gormless.'

I start slowly climbing the stairs. Unfortunately I've picked a bad time. The Year 11 assembly has just finished and I can hear them charging out of the hall. I try and go faster. I hear them reach the bottom of the stairs and start coming up.

'Slow down,' shouts some teacher at the Year 11s.

It doesn't work. The first few start going past me. Then there's more and they start barging into me. Then there are loads and I'm being knocked from side to side.

'Walk in a straight line,' says Miss Burley behind me. They all ignore her.

It feels like everybody in Year 11 wants to push past me. I feel all claustrophobic and vulnerable.

Any Year 11 kid fancying a quick crack at the back of my head could have a free shot. And kids in Year 11 at my school don't usually need any more reason than that.

Still there's only three stairs left to the top. I put on a bit of a spurt. And trip. I fall forward into the back of a Year 11 kid. He obviously thinks someone has just hit him so he shoves me back. Already off balance there isn't a lot I can do. I fall backwards into Miss Burley. I probably wouldn't have knocked her over if I hadn't been carrying a heavy box of books. But I am. So I do. And once she's falling nothing is going to stop either of us until we hit the bottom of the stairs. Which we do. First her. Then me. Then the box of books. Then the laughter of a whole yearful of unsympathetic sixteen years olds. Then...

'SHARP!'

Walton.

'WHAT ARE YOU DOING ON TOP OF MISS BURLEY?'

The Year 11's laugh even louder when he says that.

'I'm helping,' I explain.

'HELPING!' he shouts back at me. 'HELPING! THE POOR WOMAN WILL NEED MEDICAL ATTENTION. YOU BOY,' he points at random to some Year 11 kid. 'GO AND FETCH THE SCHOOL NURSE.'

This certainly gets me on my feet. It has the

same effect on Miss Burley. She's still wheezing and coughing but she's standing. I reckon the school nurse must have the same reputation with the teachers as she does with the kids. One of the first proper lessons you learn at Hanford is never ever let her come near you with a needle. Or scissors. Or even a cold flannel. She's been known to hurt kids with one of those.

'No need for that, Mr Walton,' Miss Burley tells him. 'I'll live.'

'You sure you wouldn't like a quick check from the nurse?' asks Mr Walton in a kind voice you don't hear very often.

'No.' She shakes her head vigorously.

'And you will agree with me that the state of the school stairs did nothing to contribute to your accident?' he says in a much less kind voice which you hear all the time.

'Yes,' she says but I'm not sure she knows what she's saying. Her eyes have got this glassy look.

'A verbal acknowledgement is enough,' he says, 'But I'll have my secretary draw up a formal disclaimer for you to sign later.'

He turns back to me.

'So, Sharp. What led to this debacle? Were you running? Were you descending the stairs on the left in contravention of the school one-way system? Did you drop litter and then trip over it?'

I look up into his eyes. Mr Walton has got dead

black eyes like a shark. He's looking down at me as though I'm an isolated baby dolphin that he's about to tear apart.

'He was helping me, Mr Walton.'

And just as I was about to be torn apart a kindly blue whale comes to my rescue.

'Helping you, Miss Burley. Are you sure?'

She nods.

'Really sure?'

The shark, unwilling to allow his prey to escape, tries one more time.

'Quite sure, Mr Walton.'

'Oh. Well in that case you'd better run along, Sharp. Though when I say run I don't mean it literally as that would be against school rules. I mean walk with purpose.

And so the baby dolphin was free to swim off to join his pod frolicking in the glistening coral seas of the Southern Ocean.

Or in my case, go to Resistant Materials.

Resistant Materials is a really stupid name for a subject. My mum told me that when she was at school it was called Woodwork. That makes more sense because you've got an idea what you'll be working with. Resistant Materials could be anything – wood, metal, brick or my dad's opinions.

And getting a credit in Resistant Materials is almost impossible. We've got Clayface for it. His real name is Mr Williams but everybody calls him Clayface because nobody has ever seen him smile.

'You're late,' he says to me as soon as I walk in the door.

'I was with Mr Walton,' I explain. 'There was an accident with Miss Burley and he wanted to talk to me.'

He gives me a hard look but decides to believe me.

'Coat off. Take the safety goggles and a piece of wood from my desk. Take a plane from the table by the window and stand by your bench,' he says. 'And look lively. The rest of the class is waiting.'

I do as he says. As soon as I get to my bench he starts talking to the class.

'Today we are going to do basic planeing. Watch me. Put on your safety goggles. Take the piece of wood. Place it in the vice. Hold it straight with your left hand. Approximately two centimetres of the wood should rise above the edge of the vice. Tighten the vice with your right hand by repeatedly twisting the lever clockwise until the wood is fixed in position. Pick up the plane. Hold it firmly in both hands. Place it at one end of the wood then push it smoothly down to the other end removing a layer of wood in the process. Lift up plane. Replace it at the original end of the wood. Repeat the smooth pushing movement. Continue until I say stop. Any questions?'

There aren't any.

'Right then. Get on with it. I'll be coming round to see how you're doing.'

Clayface is a tough teacher and he can usually keep our class quiet when we're not actually doing anything. But once we're all working it all falls apart pretty quickly. Yvonne Murphy says that the safety goggles are cutting into her head, Emma Roberts drops the plane on her foot and starts crying and Carolyn Edwards gets a splinter in her hand and insists she's got blood poisoning which will lead to septicaemia and gangrene – her mum's got one of those medical dictionaries. Clayface spends most of his time trying to convince the girls that they aren't seriously injured. Which leaves everybody else to do pretty much whatever they like. And what they like is chaos.

But not me. I'm after my credit. I get my piece of wood stuck in my vice and grip my plane firmly in both hands as instructed and start pushing.

'No, no, no, no, no.'

I turn round to see Clayface behind me shaking his head.

'Lad, that wood is uneven. Have you never seen a spirit level?'

'No,' I say.

'The youth of today. Get out of my way.'

I do as I'm told. He loosens the vice and pulls out the piece of wood.

'Now we'll start again. Watch me. You make sure your wood is straight in the vice. Do you see?'

I nod.

'And then and only then do you tighten the vice.'

'Right.'

'So I'll hold it to keep it straight and you tighten it.'

I move forward and start turning.

'Sir?' I ask him.

'Yes.'

'Why are we turning blocks of medium sized wood into small blocks of wood?'

'It's a basic skill.'

'But you've already got loads of small blocks of wood in the box labelled "small blocks of wood" on the table behind your desk. Why don't you just give us them to save time?'

'You've no appreciation of the National Curriculum have you, Sharp?'

He's got me there. I haven't.

'OW!'

Me and Clayface turn round. One of the morons at the back is rubbing his head and a chisel is lying suspiciously nearby on the floor. It isn't going to take Sherlock Holmes to sort out that one.

'You boy,' shouts Clayface. 'What is going on over... OW!'

Has he been hit by a chisel too?

'SHARP! STOP TURNING NOW!'

I look down. Clayface's finger is trapped in the vice. My eyes had been distracted by what had been going on with the morons but my hands had kept on with the task.

'UNDO THE VICE NOW SHARP!'

I start turning fast.

'AAARRGGH. ANTI-CLOCKWISE, YOU IDIOT.'

I turn back the other way. Clayface pulls his finger free.

'Look at what you've done.'

He holds his little finger up to my face. It's littler than it used to be. And flatter too.

That's two teachers injured and it's not even break time.

Getting this credit is going to be harder than I thought.

CHAPTER 10

I decide that I can't risk injuring another teacher. Being a detective, I know what would happen. Somebody would establish a pattern and I'd end up being regarded as a serial teacher maimer and that's the kind of reputation that can only lead to trouble.

So, for the rest of the day I turn back into myself. I don't try to get a credit and I don't try and learn too much. I take it nice 'n' easy.

Which means that when the bell goes for the end of school I'm ready to head over to the waste ground. The letter says be there at 4.15 and it's only fifteen minutes away so I've got time to stop off and buy myself a coke and a packet of prawn cocktail and eat them on the way.

I get there about ten past leaving five minutes to wait until whoever it is with their piece of information shows up. I ride over to a wall so I can lean against it without getting off my bike. The note was anonymous and I want to be able to make a quick getaway if I need to. Whoever it is, I hope they get here soon because the smell is beginning to get to me. The waste ground is next to the sewage works and that place really gives out a stink.

In fact the stench is so bad that I pinch my nose to stop smelling it. And it's really weird. I notice that I can hear things better. It's like you shut one sense down and another one starts working harder. I can hear the birds twittering, I can hear the rain splashing into the puddles and I can hear the sirens.

I wonder what will happen if I close my eyes. If blocking my nose improves my hearing then closing my eyes as well could improve it twice as much. That's the sort of thing that might come in useful one day as a detective.

Closing my eyes doesn't work quite as well as I hoped. The birds are twittering about the same level and the rain doesn't sound much louder in the puddles. But the sirens are definitely getting louder. It's odd that it works for sirens but not for birds. They keep getting louder. I can't even hear the birds any more. That doesn't make any sense. Unless of course the sirens are getting nearer.

I open my eyes. A police car is swerving off the road into the waste ground. Its brakes scream as it skids round and points itself straight at me. The engine revs and the car roars my way. Somehow I don't think my bike is going to be much use in making a getaway.

The car screeches to a stop right in front of me.

A policeman jumps out of one side of the car and a policewoman gets out of the other. They both pull out their truncheons.

'STAY EXACTLY WHERE YOU ARE,' shouts the policeman.

'DON'T MOVE,' yells the policewoman.

'WE'VE GOT YOU COVERED,' bellows the policeman.

'YOU'VE GOT NO CHANCE,' bawls the policewoman.

'GET DOWN ON THE GROUND,' orders the policeman.

'AND SPREAD YOUR ARMS AND LEGS WIDE,' adds the policewoman.

The police screaming up to you in a car and then pointing their truncheons and shouting is pretty scary. But not quite scary enough to make me get down on the ground. It's been raining non-stop for two days and the area doesn't have the best drainage.

'It's muddy,' I explain. 'I'll get my school uniform dirty.'

'ARE YOU RESISTING ARREST?' demands the policeman.

'I'm resisting mud,' I tell him. 'My mum will go mad.'

'WE'VE RECEIVED A REPORT OF A BOY MATCHING YOUR DESCRIPTION

VANDALISING THIS AREA. WHAT HAVE YOU GOT TO SAY ABOUT THAT?'

Not much.

'YOU WERE VANDALISING THIS WALL, WEREN'T YOU?'

'No.' Now seems a good time to start talking.

'YES YOU WERE.'

'No, I…'

'LOOK AT THE WRITING ABOVE YOUR HEAD.'

I look up. Along the top of the wall in blue it says,

I HATE THE POLICE. THEY ARE SC

The grafitti isn't finished but I think I get the basic idea.

'NOW LOOK AT THE GROUND TO YOUR RIGHT.'

I do what she says. Lying there is a canister of blue spray paint. I'm getting a feeling where this might all be going.

'WOULD YOU CARE TO EXPLAIN THE PHONE CALL IDENTIFYING A BOY OF YOUR DESCRIPTION VANDALISING A WALL IN CONJUNCTION WITH YOU BEING BY THE WALL WHICH WAS HALF VANDALISED ALONGSIDE A CANISTER OF SPRAY PAINT?'

'Could you repeat the question?'

'WHAT'S YOUR NAME?'

'That's a different question.'

'TELL ME YOUR NAME.'

'Mickey Sharp.'

'I AM ARRESTING YOU, MICKEY SHARP, FOR FIRST DEGREE VANDALISM. YOU DO NOT NEED TO SAY ANYTHING BUT...'

This cannot be happening.

'ANYTHING YOU DO SAY WILL BE TAKEN DOWN...'

It's still happening.

'AND USED IN EVIDENCE AGAINST YOU. NOW GET IN THE CAR.'

'But...'

'ARE YOU RESISTING ARREST?'

'I was only saying "but".'

'DO I HAVE TO CUFF YOU?'

I don't fancy that much. What if my nose starts running? There's nothing for it. I get in the police car.

CHAPTER 11

'I'm telling you, Mickey. All the evidence is against you. And it's not the first time you've been in a police station, is it?'

I shake my head. I cannot believe what has happened to me in the last two hours. First, I'm driven to the police station. Then I get dumped in an interview room. Then my mum and dad and some solicitor guy called Cochrane turn up. And now I'm going to be questioned. I can't even look at my mum and dad but I have to look at Cochrane because he keeps talking to me and he won't shut up.

'Now,' he says, 'Those police officers are going to come back into this interview room in a minute and I want you to tell them that you did what they are saying you did and say you're sorry. That way you might just get out of here with a caution. What do you say?'

'I'm innocent.'

'Do you really want to take this in front of a magistrate? They've got the phone call, they've got the canister, they've got you. It doesn't take much for someone to join the dots and before you know it you'll have an ASBO, you'll be under curfew and wearing an electronic tag.'

'But I didn't do it.'

'I'm your legal representative, Mickey. I've got your best interests at heart. Let me tell you that there aren't going to be any campaigning journalists spending time trying to overturn your conviction. There'll be no celebratory press conferences at the court of appeal. They'll just be you sitting crying in secure accommodation thinking about what might have been.'

'But I can explain. I got this anonymous note about this girl who I've been after...'

'I'm stopping you right there for your own protection,' says Cochrane, holding his hand up in the air. 'At the moment you're only looking at vandalism but you start talking crazy about being after girls and we could be looking at a stalking charge as well. Can't you make him see sense, Mr and Mrs Sharp?'

For the first time since they came into my room I risk a look at my mum and dad. I don't look for long. My mum looks like she'll never smile again and my dad looks like he'll make sure *I* never smile again.

'I'm so disappointed,' says my mum.

'I think you'd better take Mr Cochrane's advice,' says my dad. 'You're getting off lightly.'

'But I'm innocent,' I wail again.

'Stop saying that,' insists Cochrane.

'It's so ironic,' says my mum. 'Especially after this morning when I was saying that I thought we should trust him more and allow him more privacy.'

There's a small explosion in my head. I bang my hand on the table when I realise what my mum has just said.

'That's it,' I tell them.

'What?' they all say at once.

'My mum and dad were there at breakfast when I got the anonymous note telling me to go to the waste ground. If they tell the police that then the police will have to realise that I was framed.'

Cochrane suddenly looks interested.

'Could you testify to that effect, Mr and Mrs Sharp? Could you state on the stand that Mickey got an anonymous letter this morning encouraging him to be at a certain place at a certain time? Could you testify to that under oath?'

'No,' says my dad.

'Dad!' I can't believe it. I mean I know my dad has issues with stuff like me not keeping my bedroom tidy and not watching enough nature programmes but this is way too drastic a way to teach me a lesson. Refusing to be a witness for the defence of his own son.

'You'll give evidence, won't you Mum?'

'Sorry, Mickey.' She shakes her head.

I can't believe it. It's like the scene in this play we

read in English a few months ago where Caesar is betrayed by all the people who should look out for him.

Et tu, Mum.

'We can't help you because you wouldn't let us read the letter,' says my dad smugly. 'You wanted your privacy. And now you'll have all the privacy you want. In jail.'

'I'm not sure it'll come to that,' says the lawyer. 'With my legal skill I can probably keep Mickey from the big house. Perhaps we could plead mental inadequacy. Would you say Mickey could distinguish between right and wrong?'

'I'm not sure he can distinguish between right and left,' grumbles my dad.

'That isn't going to help his case,' says the lawyer.

I'm not putting up with this. I didn't do anything wrong.

'Listen,' I say. 'You're my lawyer and I'm telling you I'm innocent and we're pleading not guilty. And nobody is saying I've got mental inadequacy. Everybody would laugh at me at school. And I do know the difference between right and left. And I know the difference between left and wrong. I mean...'

The door opens and the policeman and the policewoman come back in. They sit down on the other side of the table. My lawyer sits down next to me. My parents stay sitting behind me.

'Interview recommenced at 17.30 hours,' says the policewoman.

'Mickey,' says the policeman. 'Are you prepared to admit that you were vandalising the wall?'

'My client is still thinking about that,' says the lawyer.

'No, I didn't,' I say.

'As your lawyer I strongly advise you not to answer that question,' he says.

'As Mickey Sharp, I strongly advise you to get lost.'

There's a long silence after I say that.

Eventually the policeman breaks it.

'You'd better take him home,' he tells my mum and dad. 'We're getting nowhere here. I'll review the case with my sergeant and we'll charge him tomorrow.'

That doesn't sound good.

'Interview terminated at 17.32.'

CHAPTER 12

It only takes ten minutes to get home according to the clock in our car but it feels like a whole lot longer. My mum and dad have had to drive me home from a police station once before but it's not one of those things that gets easier. The silence is filled with bitterness and disappointment.

'Go to your room,' says my mum as soon as we get home.

'Get into bed and stay there,' adds my dad. 'I don't want to see or hear you until tomorrow morning. Your mother and I are going to drink whisky and try to work out where it all went wrong.'

I was hoping that's what they'd say. I go straight to my room.

But I am not going to bed. I need to get back to that waste ground and find some way of proving myself innocent. And when I've done that I can try to solve this case. It didn't mean that much before but now it's personal. Somebody wants to stop me getting to Desiree bad enough to get me arrested.

There must be some very big stuff indeed at stake here.

The first thing I do is wait five minutes to let them get settled with their drinks and their criticisms. Then very carefully I inch my way along the landing. The stairs are too creaky to walk on so I climb onto the banister and lower myself down it little by little. One slip and I'd come crashing down in a noisy heap but I've been down this banister many times before and the only thing that can go wrong is an unexpected splinter. Otherwise I'm fine.

But there's a problem when I get to the bottom of the stairs. The door to the lounge is open. I can't believe it. The lounge door is never open. My dad has got this thing about draughts. His theory is that if you keep all doors and windows shut at all times then you'll only ever need to put the heating on once a week. The problem is that if you never opened any doors you'd never be able to get out of the house so you'd never get to the shops so that in the end you'd starve to death. But you would die with very low heating bills which, according to my dad, is a deal worth considering.

So the door being open can't be accidental. They must have left it open deliberately to block off my escape route. I'm trapped.

I climb back up the stairs to the landing and tiptoe back to my room. Carefully I ease open my bedroom window and take a look out. Every film you ever see gives you the idea that every kid's bedroom is conveniently located next to a gnarled old tree with loads of branches. This tree is used for one of two things. If it's a horror film then it's always bashing its branches against the window during storms just before the ghost/monster/axe-wielding maniac appears and if it's a soppy film about kids doing something a little bit naughty then the kid uses it to climb out of to go off with his friends and save the cute space alien.

But real life isn't like that.

There's nothing outside my window. Just a straight drop.

But there are no other options.

I haul myself up until I'm sitting on my window ledge. Then I swing my legs out and carefully I begin to turn myself around so that I'm supporting myself with my hands and looking into my bedroom. I start to lower myself. My chest drops below the window sill. Then my neck.

I lower myself until I'm hanging by the tips of my fingers.

Now comes the difficult bit.

Letting go.

I count to three. Then I decide that three isn't a particularly good number so I count to ten instead. Then I figure that maybe I was discriminating unfairly against three so I add another three. Then I realise that I've got to thirteen. That's the last number anybody wants to have counted to before they let go of a window sill. So, I take away four because I've always liked the number nine. Then I feel stupid for doing mental arithmetic at such an inappropriate moment. Then my arms decide this has all been going on too long and let go without my brain's permission.

I'm falling. I'm…

Bang. I'm in a heap on the ground.

I check to see if I'm still alive. I am.

I'm really glad I 'forgot' to mow the lawn last weekend because the grass cushioned my landing. Which shows you should always think twice about doing jobs that your parents ask you to do.

I grab my bike and head to the front gate. I've still got to get past the lounge window so I have to crawl along the ground pushing my bike in front of me to make sure that I'm not seen. Then, as soon as I'm past it, I leap onto my bike and peddle like anything to get to the waste ground.

As soon as I get there, I head straight over to the wall. The graffiti is exactly the same as when I left it. When I look at it now the blue bit about the police seems really obvious knowing what I know. Back then it looked like all the other bits of graffiti.

There's nothing else. No clue as to who might really have done it.

I'm doomed.

'You again.'

I turn round. Approaching me from the other side of the waste ground is a woman with red hair. She's carrying a telescope and a camera. And a really angry expression as well.

And I thought today couldn't get any worse.

'What are you doing?' she says.

'I'm looking at the wall.'

'Why?'

I shrug. I don't really fancy getting into a discussion with her.

'It probably won't matter to you but I was looking at that wall myself. I was looking at it for a rare foreign migrant – the Spanish starling. It's a bird. It was here earlier today. You may care to know that the Spanish starling has never been photographed in the wild in Britain. I would have been the envy of twitchers everywhere if I could have snapped it. It was just settling on this wall and then you appeared and scared it off.'

I shrug again. I feel like telling her that if she thinks she's got problems when all that is wrong is that she can't get a picture of a bird then she should try being me. I'll be wearing an electronic tag by next week.

'My day has been ruined,' she says. 'The Spanish starling isn't coming back.'

She turns to go.

'Wait,' I say suddenly.

'What is it?'

I'm not sure. It's something she said but I can't put my finger on it.

'Is it a bird?' she says, 'Or are you being a pain?'

I've got it.

'No it's "again",' I shout.

'What?' she says.

'You said "again".'

'Did I?' She doesn't sound very sure.

'Yes,' I tell her. 'You said, "You again" when you saw me.'

'Look,' she says. 'I understand that you live a very boring life. You must do if you spend your time looking at walls. And so reliving the highlights of conversations you've recently been involved in is probably something you find quite stimulating. I understand that. But I have a life. I have to go now.'

She turns away again and start walking off. I can't let her go. I cycle round in front of her.

'Get out of the way,' she tells me.

'You don't understand,' I say. 'When you said "again" that means you saw me before when I was taken away by the police.'

'And a great service that was to birdwatching,' she says. 'You scared the Spanish starling off last time you came too.'

'But they arrested me for vandalism. They say I was spraying paint on the wall and if you saw me then you know it's not true. You can go and tell them and then they won't put me under a curfew.'

'A curlew?' .

'No, a curfew,' I say again. 'It means I can't go out.'

'And a good thing too,'

'But you must have seen that I didn't do anything,' I say.

'Suppose I did,' she says. 'What should I do about it?'

I can't believe how stupid adults can be sometimes.

'Tell the police,' I say. 'Be my alibi.'

'Why?'

'Because then I'll be free.'

'Free to scare more rare migrants,' she says. 'I don't think so. Goodbye.'

I can't believe it. I've actually found someone who could prove my innocence and she won't help.

'What if I promise never to scare another bird again ever?'

She doesn't even look back. I'm so frustrated. I close my eyes and make one of those noises that you make when everything has nearly gone really right and then just at the last moment has gone really wrong.

'Aaarrrgghh.'

It doesn't make me feel any better. I open my eyes. She's turned round and is staring at me.

'Make that noise again.'

'You mean, "Aaarrrrgghh,' I say.

'It's uncanny.' She looks really excited

'What?'

'That noise is an almost faultless reproduction of the mating cry of the male Spanish starling.'

'How do you know?' I ask.

'It's exactly like the CD I've got at home.'

They make CD's of bird's mating songs and people buy them? Every time you find out something new about the world it makes it seem a stranger place.

'Now,' she says, 'the Spanish starling I'm attempting to photograph just so happens to be a female. If you were to reproduce that noise there is a possibility that the bird may show itself for a sufficient amount of time for me to focus and shoot. I would have my picture for the Birding Gazette and you wouldn't feel as bad as you probably do at the moment for making my afternoon a complete waste of time.'

'I don't feel that bad,' I tell her.

'Well, you should.'

'But I don't,' I say. 'Because I've got too many of my own problems to worry about. But if you were to tell me that if you got the picture then the first thing you would do would be to go down to the police station and tell them that I didn't vandalise the wall. Then I might feel differently.'

She thinks about it for a moment.

'All right. You've got a deal.'

'Aaarrrgghh,' I say happily.

I just hope the Spanish starling is feeling romantic.

CHAPTER 13

Ten minutes later and I'm cycling home. The Spanish starling was obviously feeling very romantic because it appeared almost straight away. After all the effort to attract it I was expecting something a bit special but it was a bit of a let down as birds go, being drab and black and nothing else. All the birds in Hanford are like that. Not like the birds you see on nature documentaries that are all different colours. Even the robin that you see in our garden around Christmas has got a grey breast. I figure that Hanford must be the centre of the world for dull birds. It didn't bother the woman though. She took about a hundred photos of it and I went 'Aaarrgghh,' for so long that I thought my throat was going to dry up. While I was croaking I realised that I hadn't asked her whether she could give me a description of who had done the vandalism. Fortunately she ran out of film before I ran out of voice but when I asked, she couldn't help. She'd got there only about ten minutes before I did.

So, I don't know who was trying to set me up

but I do know that I should be free of the police. She headed straight off to the station after the last of the photos to put things right.

Now, my plan is to sneak back into the house through the back door if I can and try to get up to my bedroom. Then I can wait until I hear the telephone ring which will be the police dropping all the charges. As soon as I hear the phone ring I'll make my face look like I've been crying and then when my mum and dad come upstairs to tell me the good news they'll feel so bad for thinking that I was guilty in the first place that they'll let me get away with everything for at least a month.

Some people might think that treating your parents like that is bad and wrong but one thing I've learnt in life is that you should always get as much out of the situation as you can when the cards are falling for you because you always have to pay when they aren't.

I crawl back under the lounge window safely enough and slip into the back garden. I'm about to head over to the back door when I notice something moving outside my shed.

I head down to check it out. Standing there listening to a walkman and looking very bored is DJ Smarty aka Jenni's little brother.

'Where have you been?' he demands. 'You told me to meet you here after school and I got here and waited and you never showed so I went home for my tea and then I came back and you still weren't here.'

With all the hassle of the police and trying to prove I was innocent I'd forgotten all about him.

'There was nothing I could do,' I tell him. 'I was arrested.'

'Really?' he looks impressed.

'Yeah,' I say. 'They were trying to fit me up but I made bail and found myself an alibi.'

I know it sounds like a bad American cop show but it's better than 'my parents brought me home and then I went out and convinced a birdwatcher help me out by doing impressions of a mating Spanish starling.'

'That's really cool,' he says. And then he remembers that he's supposed to be a tough guy himself so he adds, 'of course that kind of thing is happening to me all the time so I know how it is.'

I nod sympathetically. This is no time to laugh at him.

'What do we do next?' he says.

'I have a plan,' I tell him.

'What is it?'

'It's secret.'

The thing about a plan is that you should never tell anybody about it. Because if you do they automatically find something wrong with it. They never say that it's the most perfect plan they've ever heard of and it's certain to work. So, you end up having an argument about whether your plan will or won't work instead of actually trying it out which in the end is the only way to know.

'But I'm working with you,' he says. 'We're partners.'

I stop that one straight off. No eleven year old is going to be allowed to go round telling people that he's my partner.

'We are not partners,' I tell him. 'You have a temporary role as my assistant.'

'But I don't want to be an assistant,' he says. 'It sounds rubbish. I want a proper title or I'm going to tell my sister to take the case off you.'

This is getting irritating. I try to think of some title I can give him that will shut him up. Trouble is I don't really know anything about titles unless it's queen or duke or something and I can't give him one of those. The only other people I know who have job titles are teachers. Some of them are just teachers but then there're others who are Deputy Heads or Heads of Year or Directors of Studies. You see it on their office doors when you're sent there for behaving badly by the teachers who actually do the work. I try and remember any other good titles.

'I know,' I tell him as one jumps into my mind. 'You can be the Clues Co-ordinator.'

'Clues Co-ordinator.' he says with a smile. ' I like that. That sounds good.'

It sounds good but it doesn't mean anything. Just like our school's anti-bullying policy.

'MICKEY!'

It's my mum. And she's shouting. I'm guessing that I've been rumbled for not being in my bedroom. I don't want to run into her yet.

'Quick,' I say to Smarty. 'Hide.'

We slip behind the shed but it's too late.

'MICKEY! I SAW YOU GO BEHIND THAT SHED. DON'T MAKE ME COME DOWN THERE.'

There's nothing for it. I'm going to have to go and talk to her.

'Wait here,' I tell Smarty, 'I'll be back as soon as I can.'

Which depending on what's been going on elsewhere could be a minute or could be tomorrow.

My mum is standing on the back step. She never goes into the garden if she can avoid it. You'd think it was mined.

'Hi, Mum,' I say.

'Don't say "Hi, Mum," to me' she snaps. 'Why aren't you in your room?'

Things don't look good.

'You see, Mum, there was something that I had to do straight...'

'Nothing is more important than doing exactly what your father and I tell you to do when we tell you to do it.'

I think I can say bye-bye to my career as a detective for a while.

'We have to fetch you from the police station where you are under arrest for vandalism and even then you won't do what we say. You'll be very lucky if you are allowed out at all until you're eighteen when we'll throw you out and rent your room to a student.'

'But. Mum...'

'In fact the only thing that could save you from that is if the police had just rung to say that a woman has come forward and told them that you had nothing to do with vandalising anything and that therefore they will not be proceeding with any charges.'

'But, Mum, listen, please...'

And then I realise what she just said. I look at her face. She's smiling. You don't see my mum smile much these days.

'I'm so pleased, Mickey,' she says. 'I didn't want to believe that you'd done what the police said you had but they seemed so sure.'

I don't say I told you so. Never kick your mother when she's down.

'But that doesn't explain why you're out here in the garden when you should be in your bedroom.'

I was hoping that in her delight at my innocence she wouldn't notice that.

'Well, Mickey?'

'You see, Mum...'

'Yes, Mickey.'

'You see, Mum, I knew that I hadn't done it and because of my complete belief in British justice I knew that I would be cleared. And then I thought that you and Dad would feel terrible because you'd believed all these bad things about me and you'd feel even worse because you'd punished me unfairly. And I didn't want that to be on your conscience. So I decided to ignore you. It was for your own good.'

My mum tries to work out exactly what it is I've said. I hope I've made it confusing enough for it to be too difficult.

'So,' she says after a few seconds. 'You're telling me that you disobeyed our specific instructions to make us feel better.'

Unfortunately I didn't make it too difficult.

'That's about it,' I tell her.

'Mickey. You...' and then she stops. 'Oh, who cares. Ten minutes ago my son was a criminal. Now he's just not doing what I tell him. I'll take that.'

And she smiles which, I think, means that it's going to be all right. And then she kisses me.

'Mum,' I tell her pulling back. 'People can see.'

You've got to stop your mum kissing you in public straight away because if you let them get away with it once they might keep doing it. They forget that you're not five any more and that you've got a reputation to look after.

'I won't mention where I found you to your father,' says my mum. 'He's not quite as good as me at making compromises with reality.'

I don't know what that means but it sounds like my dad.

'I've got to go, mum,' I tell her.

'You always do, Mickey.'

And then she gives me that look. It's a look that your mum gives you sometimes and you can see her remembering when you were a really tiny baby who just puked and cried and who couldn't do anything without her help. It's the sort of look that you find yourself looking away from fast.

'See you later,' I say and I head off down to the shed where Smarty is waiting but I can feel her watching me all the time I'm walking away. Maybe I should look back but I don't.

CHAPTER 14

'What's the matter with your mum?' says Smarty when I get back to the shed. 'She's just there doing nothing.'

'We don't need to talk about my mother,' I tell him I look at my watch. It's almost seven o'clock 'We're going to be late so come on.'

'Where are we going?'

'You'll know when we get there.'

But before we can leave the shed door opens. Umair walks in.

'All right?' he says.

I'm surprised. It's almost a year since he's been round to my house. I nod.

'Who's this?' demands DJ Smarty.

'This is Umair.'

'What does he want?'

Normally I'd tell an eleven year old that he didn't talk like that in my shed but since I want to know the answer too I let it ride.

'I've come to help,' he says. 'With that thing you were talking about this morning.'

That's what good about Umair. He's not stupid enough to blurt out my plan until he knows who this other kid is.

'But I thought you had a chess game?'

He looks a bit awkward when I say that. But then again I suppose if playing chess was a large part of your social life you probably wouldn't want smart-mouthed eleven year olds hearing about it.

'He ended up stuck in a Fried Liver Attack,' he mumbles. 'It was carnage.'

This must mean something in the chess world but it means nothing to me. And every second that we waste the queue downtown is getting longer.

'Come on,' I tell them.

We hit a problem as soon as we get outside though. I've got a bike. So has Umair. Smarty's got nothing.

'I'm a rapper,' he says. 'I ain't using no bike. I'm waiting for a Porsche.'

If he's waiting for a Porsche around my area, he's got a long wait. But I can't leave him. Right away he'd be on the mobile to Jenni telling her that I wasn't solving the case and she'd pull me off it. And I don't want that. Especially in front of Umair. I don't want the first thing he sees of my detective work to be me getting the sack.

'Get on my bike,' I tell Smarty.

He climbs on reluctantly and we ride. You have to work harder when you've got someone sitting behind you even if they are little like Smarty. You have to sort of stand up on the pedals which means that your thighs hurt a bit, but I do a lot of cycling so it isn't too bad.

'This isn't a very smooth ride,' Smarty complains as we freewheel down Chamberlain Avenue.

'The brakes don't seem to work too well,' he comments as we make a rather sudden stop at the Hunter's Way traffic lights.

'I didn't think they made bikes with as few gears as yours,' is his final observation as we head down Forum Road to the Hanford Colosseum.

I just grit my teeth and ignore him. It still annoys me though. I'm a bit sensitive where my bike is concerned and I still haven't got over that phone he's got.

But the sight of the queue takes my mind off it. We see the back of it before we even see the Colosseum and that's the biggest building in the whole of Hanford. We ride past it. It's a massive long line. And it's screaming. And because the queue is all girls about eight years old the screams are very squeaky. It sounds like the whole town has been overrun by mice. But instead of cheese these mice want:

'GIRL POWER. WE WANT GIRL POWER. WE WANT GIRL POWER.'

They keep the chant up all the time we're riding past them. I can't believe it. Two days ago almost none of them would have even heard of Girl Power. But all it takes is one appearance on The Hits Show and it's like they can't live without them.

'What are we doing here?' demands Smarty from behind me.

'If we're going to get Desiree back then we're going to have to go to where we know she's going to be,' I say. I try and sound confident as I say it but I've got to be honest the sight of all these kids screaming has got me worried. How am I ever going to get her away from all this fame and back to being nothing more than a wannabe in the Really Tough Crew?

'How are we going to get her back then?' says Smarty. That's typical of him – asking the question I don't think I can answer.

'Watch and learn,' I tell him. It doesn't mean anything but Mr Stubbs, out art teacher, says it every now and again when I ask him how to paint something. He either says that or he shakes his head and says my work lacks inspiration and horses. I don't know why but he thinks every painting I do could be improved by adding a horse. Even the one that was supposed to be on the moon.

'Let's dump the bikes,' I say.

That's one of the good things about bikes. You can ride them right up to the door of where you want to go and lock them to the nearest lamp post. It doesn't take long.

'What do we do now?' says Smarty when we've got rid of the bikes.

I look at the queue. It's very long. If we join it then the chances of us getting in are non-existent. The Colosseum is a big place but there's no way all this lot are going to fit in. If only I hadn't got into trouble with the police then I'd have been here in plenty of time but now thanks to all that I'm going to have to try something else to get in.

Like the stage door!

At Christmas, my Uncle Brendan used to take me and my sister to see pantomimes at the Hanford Colosseum. One year my sister decided she wanted the handsome prince's autograph so after the show we went down a narrow street, which you'd never normally notice, where the stage door was. We had to wait for about an hour before the actors came out and then, when my sister saw the prince without his make-up on, she decided that he wasn't that good looking after all and she didn't want his autograph so we'd done all that waiting for nothing.

But if actors come out that way then we can get in that way too.

'Come on,' I say to Umair and Smarty.

I head off down to the side street with them following me. And I've remembered right – the stage door there. It's strange when you look at it. It's a really normal door, in fact it's even a bit drab and the green paint is peeling off it but it's this door that all the stars and celebrities go through whereas the normal people like me get to go through the fancy main doors.

But when we get close there's something there that I don't remember from before. It's locked. What that means is that there's no way that I'm going to be able to sneak in to see Desiree. But there's an intercom. I'm going to have to talk my way into getting buzzed in. And then just when I'm thinking about what I might say Umair points his finger upwards. There's a CCTV camera trained on the door entrance too. That makes things even harder.

I motion to the other two to back off.

'One of us might be able to get in here,' I tell them once we're far enough away to be out of sight, 'but we need to come up with a good reason. Any ideas?'

'If I had an Ouzi or an AK-45,' says Smarty, 'I'd blow the doors and we'd be in there real fast.'

'It's an AK-47,' points out Umair.

'I knew that,' bristles DJ Smarty. 'I was just testing y'all, to see if you were hip to the kinds of hardware that are out on the street.'

If he lives in Hanford-on-the-Hill, the only hardware out on his streets are golf clubs.

'I think we need something a bit more subtle,' I say. 'Assault weapons tend to draw attention to themselves.'

'Yeah man, but smaller guns aren't going to get the job done,' counters DJ Smarty.

'I was thinking about not using guns at all,' I tell him. 'I was thinking about using my brain.'

DJ Smarty looks doubtful.

'The last time you used your brain it didn't get us very far. Maybe your brain needs to rest a while until it's recovered its strength.'

'A delivery,' says Umair out of nowhere.

'What?'

'That's how you get in places. You deliver things to them. Then people open the door to let you in.'

'None of us look like postmen,' says DJ Smarty.

Umair shakes his head.

'It doesn't have to be letters, does it? Loads of other things get delivered.'

'Like what?' I ask.

'Like pizzas,' answers DJ Smarty even though I was talking to Umair. 'And Desiree loves pizzas. I was hanging with the crew one day and she had an American Beast with extra salami for lunch and a five cheeses for tea.'

'Five cheeses?' I say. 'I thought you could only get four.'

'She adds Dairylea to hers,' explains DJ Smarty.

Unusual. Still it's worth a try.

'Get over there, man,' says DJ Smarty. 'Hit the intercom and tell them that you're delivering a pizza to Desiree. They'll buzz you in right away.'

113

I don't like the way he's giving the orders here. This is supposed to be my show. But we haven't got much time and it's the only idea going.

'What about the CCTV?' says Umair. 'They'll see he hasn't got a pizza and they won't let him in.'

'Good point, man. We're going to have to get him a pizza.'

'Where are...' I begin to say because I feel like I'm losing control of everything right now, but Umair cuts me off.

'He doesn't need a pizza. He needs a pizza box. That's all they need to see.'

'You're right, man. It's good to see your brain is working.'

This is really beginning to annoy me.

'Where do you get a pizza box except in a pizza place?' I tell them. 'What are we going to do? Go in and ask for an empty box?'

'Could we get a side order of garlic bread with it?' asks DJ Smarty. 'I really like garlic bread.'

'Don't be stupid,' I tell him. 'Anyway there isn't a pizza place around here.'

'But there is a bin,' says Umair indicating the bottom of the street. He's right. There is a bin. It's one of those huge ones that they call dumpsters on American cop shows which are as big as the skip outside our next door neighbour's house.

I see where he's going. It's worth a look.

'Come on,' I say quickly to show I'm still in charge.

We head down to the bin. It's even bigger when we get next to it. You can't see over the top to see what's in it. I turn to DJ Smarty.

'You're the smallest,' I tell him. 'We'll lift you up and you can check it out.'

'No way,' says DJ Smarty. 'I don't do bins. It's your case. We'll lift you up.'

'You're too weak.'

'No I'm not. I work out. I've got a six pack.'

'They're probably your ribs,' I tell him but it doesn't make any difference. He isn't going to do it. Which means one thing.

'Lift me up then,' I tell them with a sigh.

I think Umair takes most of my weight but they still manage to get me up high enough so I can see into the bin. And smell into it too which is one sensory experience more than I needed. But my eyes tell me that there's a big red and white pizza box on the top.

'Keep hold of my legs,' I shout down to them. 'I'm going to reach down and get one.'

I figure everybody in the entire world except me knew what was going to happen next. The pizza box is just out of reach. I make an effort to reach out those extra couple of centimetres. Just as I get a firm grip on the box I hear a cry of 'Woah!' from DJ Smarty and feel one of my legs come free. There's a shout of 'Aargh!' from Umair as his grip loosens too and I slide forward. The pizza box isn't joining me. I'm joining it.

'Uuugghh.'

The smell is disgusting. I mean really disgusting. And it's not just the smell. My face has landed in something wet and rotten.

'Mickey? Are you okay?'

I've got to get out of here. I try to stand up. I'm almost there when my leg gives way underneath me and I flop backwards and splat into something nasty again. Straight away I'm back up but it's hard to keep my balance. It's like trying to stand up in stinky quicksand – everywhere you put your feet moves and burps.

'Mickey?'

I manage to poke my head over the top of the bin.

'Are you okay?' says Umair.

'You've got a chip stuck in your hair,' says DJ Smarty.

I reach up and pull it out. I wish the person who bought it hadn't been such a fan of ketchup.

'Chuck out the pizza box,' says Umair.

The last thing I want to do is to stick my head back down among all the garbage below me but there are times in a detective's career when he's just got to hold his nose and get the dirty bit of the business done.

I pull out the pizza box and chuck it out of the dumpster.

'Hey! Watch it!' shouts DJ Smarty because it lands on his head.

That's about the only thing that's happened in the last few minutes that I'm not sorry about.

I climb out after it. Umair and Smarty both take a few steps backwards.

'You stink,' says Smarty.

'Thanks,' I tell him. 'Any more useful information you got, why don't you keep it to yourself?'

'I will,' says DJ Smarty. 'I'm sorry I ever told you about the chip on your head. Without me it would have stayed there for the rest of your life.'

I ignore him and take a look at myself. My hoodie is all messed up from being in the dumpster but my jeans aren't too bad. If I take my hoodie off then maybe with just a clean t-shirt I can still cut it as a pizza delivery man. As my hoodie's already messed up I use it to wipe whatever rotten gunk has got stuck to my face.

'How do I look?' I ask Umair.

He shrugs.

'You need a baseball cap,' he says. 'Pizza delivery men always have a baseball cap.'

We both look at DJ Smarty. He starts shaking his head real fast.

'No, no, no, no, no,' he says. 'This baseball cap is limited edition in America and totally unavailable in this country. There ain't no way that I'm going to let it get in contact with his greasy tomato ketchup covered head. You get what I'm saying?'

We get what he's saying. But we also get something far more important. We're fourteen and he's eleven and there are two of us and one of him.

Less than a minute later, I'm buzzing on the intercom wearing his limited-edition-unavailable-in-this-country baseball cap and I don't even care if I'm getting ketchup on it.

'Who is it?' says a woman's voice.

'Pizza,' I say.

'Who for?' says the voice.

'Desiree from Power Girl or something.' I deliberately get it muddled up so that she doesn't think I'm a crazy fan. 'It's an American Beast with extra salami.' That's got to convince her.

'Don't these young girls ever think about their complexions?' says the woman. 'OK, I'm buzzing you in. Push the door.'

I do as she says. I can't believe it. I'm in.

CHAPTER 15

In front of me is a flight of stairs. I go straight up. I figure Desiree must be due on stage soon so I need to be quick.

But my luck runs out at the top of the stairs. There's a desk and a woman sitting at it. She's got these big glasses and earrings on and long black hair with grey streaks. She looks a bit like a witch.

'You can leave the pizza there,' she says. 'Someone will be along in a moment to take it to the artiste.'

This wasn't exactly what I'd planned on. What I'd planned on was being told where Desiree was so I could take the pizza to her. I need a reason not to just hand over the pizza and walk out. I resort to plan B. Which is...

'Is there a toilet I could use?'

'I beg your pardon.'

'A toilet. I'm desperate for a...'

'I don't need any more information thank you. I suppose you can use the lavatory for the backstage staff. Go down the corridor and turn left. It has a blue

119

door. Do not on any account use the toilet with the red door. That is reserved for the artistes.'

'Thanks,' I say as I turn to go. Going to the toilet never fails.

'Haven't you forgotten something?'

I turn back.

'What?'

'The pizza.'

I look down. I was about to take the box away with me.

'Oh yeah.'

I haven't got any choice. I put the pizza box on her desk and run off down the corridor towards the toilet.

'Don't be too long,' she shouts from behind me.

I go round the corner so that I'm out of sight. I head past the blue door and then the red door and turn into another corridor. It's totally the opposite of the bits of the Colosseum that you normally see. All the paint is peeling off the walls and there's loose wires hanging down from the ceiling. I walk past a woman who's saying 'Five minutes everybody please' and I pass a guy in a suit. I'm trying not to walk too slowly so that I attract attention and not too fast so that I miss Desiree. The trouble is I don't know where she'll be. In my head I'm hoping that I spot a door with a big star on it because she's bound to be in there but in another part of my head I'm not too sure that dressing rooms really do have stars stuck on them. I turn into another corridor. And then another. A couple of women go by me but I don't recognise either of them from The Hits Show. I turn into another corridor and as I do I hear a shout,

'You cow.'

I've found Girl Power.

At the end of the corridor is a big room. Inside it I can see them all. And they're all shouting.

'Don't call her a cow.'

'I'll call her what I like. She stole my solo.'

'You can't get the high notes.'

'Yes I can, fat girl.'

'Don't call her fat.'

'She is fat. She's a size 10.'

'I'd be a size 8 if I was a dwarf like you.'

'I need to grate some cheese. Can I use your face?'

'They're clearing up. It was an allergic reaction.'

'Stay at the back of the stage. You don't want to scare off our fans.'

'What do you mean our fans? You haven't got any fans. I get way more fan mail than you.'

'Only because you send it to yourself.'

'At least I can write.'

Now I've walked into some dodgy situations before when it's been the only way to solve a case but I've got to admit that my legs really don't want to walk down the corridor. Don't get me wrong. I've seen girls fight before. On Valentine's Day all you see at break time in our school is girls trying to scratch each other's faces with their nails and pulling hair. But walking in among five at once is going to take some nerve. And I'm not really sure I've got it.

'You might be able to write but you can't spell.'

'I can spell M...I...N...G...E...R which is all I need if I want to write to you.'

'I can't believe you're talking. I thought you only used your mouth for stuffing chocolate in.'

'Not like you. You never get a chance to eat because there's always a boy's tongue down your throat.'

These girls really know how to dish out the insults and I get the feeling they won't suddenly decide to become all friendly just because I show up. But there isn't any other way. I start walking.

'If we weren't about to go onstage I'd have you.'

'You slap her you'll have to slap me too.'

'That won't be no trouble.'

I get to the door. They're enjoying their screaming match way too much to notice me. I take a deep breath and I knock on the doorframe. They don't notice. I knock again. They still don't notice so I kick it. Finally they notice.

It's quite nerve-wracking having five very angry girl pop stars all staring at you. I try to give them a smile.

'What?' they all say at once.

It's now or never.

'Would it be okay to talk to Desiree for a minute?'

My voice just has to pick this moment to let me down. It's breaking at the moment. I mean it's already broken. It's just that once or twice a week it forgets that it's broken and one sentence comes out like I've inhaled a balloon full of helium.

'What did he say?'

'You mean squeaked.'

They all start laughing. Isn't it nice of me to make these girls, who ten seconds ago all hated each other, friends again? It gives me a warm feeling all over.

This time I concentrate really hard on keeping my voice low.

'Can I speak to...'

Just as I'm about to say Desiree I feel a heavy hand clamp down hard on my shoulder and twist. I find myself face to face with a guy with huge biceps and a small head.

'I got a call from the backstage manageress,' he says. 'She tells me that some pizza delivery boy left a pizza with her and went off to the toilet. She checked the pizza to see if the anchovies were satisfactorily distributed and do you know what she found?'

'No,' I say.

'She found that there were no anchovies at all. In fact there were no anchovies, no olives, no salami and no capers. There wasn't even a base. What do you think there was?'

'I don't know.'

'There was nothing. So she checks the toilet but he isn't there. In fact he isn't anywhere. So they put the walkie-talkie message through to me because I'm Peter Peterson of Peterson's Personal Privacy Protection and I'm the kind of man who protects stars like these good ladies here from unpleasant individuals like you.'

'Oh,' I say.

'And I get straight down here and what do I find but you about to invade the personal space of these girls. Well let me tell you something. Nobody invades nobody else's personal space on my watch.'

'You're invading mine,' I point out.

'You don't count,' he tells me. 'Now have any of you ladies been distressed or upset by this individual?'

'He squeaked at us.'

'It was awful.'

'Did you squeak at these girls?'

'No.'

'He did. He did.'

'Well okay, I did but I didn't mean anything by it.'

'Now you're changing your story. What are you? Some kind of weirdo. Sneaking into theatres and squeaking at nice girls like these.'

'No, I...'

'Are you some kind of terrorist?'

'He's a terrorist. He's a terrorist.'

'I'm not a terrorist.'

'You're coming with me,' says Peter Peterson. 'You do a good show, girls. And don't you worry about weirdoes like this one. Peter Peterson of Peterson's Personal Privacy Protection ensures that Popstars Produce Pleasing Performances.'

'Wow!' say the girls, impressed by his muscles as he drags me off by the neck.

'Ow,' I say. I could live without his muscles. They're hurting me.

He drags me down all the corridors, past the red door, past the blue door, past the backstage manageress (where we stop briefly so she can bang me on the head with an empty pizza box), down the stairs and through the stage door where I'm chucked forward and I land in a puddle.

'And stay out,' says Peter Peterson before slamming the door behind me.

I hear feet running over to me and I lift my head up. Looking down at me are Umair and DJ Smarty.

'Did something go wrong then?' asks DJ Smarty.

I sigh and put my head back in the puddle.

CHAPTER 16

'Another letter, Mickey,' says my mum, dropping an envelope down on the kitchen table.

It's the next morning and I'm eating my muesli.

'Why does he get letters when I don't?' says Karen. 'I'm older than him. I should get letters.'

'What's this about letters?' says my dad coming in from the lounge where he'd been watching a programme about termites on BBC2.

'Mickey's got a letter,' repeats my mum.

'We should have email,' says Karen. 'All my friends are on the web.'

'A letter?' says my dad.

'One girl in my class got invited to a party in Amsterdam,' says Karen. 'That's the kind of thing I'm missing out on because we aren't online.'

'Let's have a look at this letter,' says my dad.

'Only if Mickey says it's okay,' says my mum.

'We're not going to go through this whole privacy nonsense again, are we?'

'It's not nonsense. The children are getting older.

We need to respect their boundaries. Soon they'll be off to college.'

'Or jail.'

'I thought we'd agreed that wasn't Mickey's fault. He was the victim of a hoax.'

'Exactly. A hoax that started with him getting a letter that he wouldn't show us. Which is why he should show us this time.'

'We can't withdraw his right to privacy because he was a victim of some stupid prank.'

'We have to protect him from himself.'

'That's what the parents of my friend said,' remarks Karen. 'when they wouldn't let her go to the party in Amsterdam.'

'I'm not wasting any more time on this,' says my dad shaking his head. 'If you aren't willing to protect your son from himself then I suppose you'll have to accept the consequences. I've got to go and watch A Year in the Life of the Sea Cucumber. There are more of these nature documentaries on than you think.'

'I've got to blow dry my hair,' says Karen.

'Is that the time?' says my mum. 'I'm going to be late for work.

They all leave the kitchen. I haven't said a word.

I look at the envelope. It's exactly the same as the one that I got yesterday. Maybe I shouldn't open it. The last one got me into so much trouble that it might be better just to throw this one away. But there's two things stopping me. The first is that the last message referred to the case and even though it didn't lead anywhere last time it might do this time, and the second is that it's almost impossible not to open an envelope with your name on it.

So, I open it.

SORRY ABOUT YESTERDAY. IT WAS TOO
DANGEROUS. PETERSON WAS WATCHING
ME. IF YOU WANT TO KNOW HOW TO GET TO
DESREE BE STANDING BY THE LAKE IN
HANFORD PARK AT TWELVE FORTY FIVE.
  A FRIEND.

I was all set to throw it into the bin but I can't. I'm hooked. 'Peterson was watching me.' I know who Peterson is. He's the security bloke for Girl Power. That means that whoever is writing these letters is very close to Girl Power – they might even be in Girl Power. Maybe a pop star is writing to me. She signs herself a friend. Maybe she wants to be more than a friend. Maybe…

I'm getting carried away. I'm imagining that there's some pop star chasing after me and I'm forgetting that last night I watched them all yelling at each other. None of them looked like they were the kind of girl that it would be any fun to go out with.

And there's a big chance it's a trap. It's too big a

coincidence to believe that someone just happened to call the police and that there just happened to be a can of spray paint lying on the floor near some half-finished graffiti. And who was the only person who knew that I'd be by that wall at that time?

The person who wrote that note.

No. What I should do is treat that letter in the way that it deserves which is to tear into as many pieces as I can and chuck it in the bin.

Instead, I put it in my pocket.

My dad comes back into the kitchen.

'Did you know that the sea cucumber can…'

I figure that it's time to go to school.

There's nothing much happening when I get there but then there never is. I head to registration and sit down next to Umair.

'Hi,' I say.

'Hi,' he says.

'My dad's watching a documentary on sea cucumbers,' I tell him.

He grunts. I suppose it isn't exactly the most thrilling way to start a conversation.

'I got another anonymous letter,' I say which is definitely better.

'Another one?' he says. 'I didn't know you'd had one.'

'Didn't I tell you?'

He shakes his head.

So I tell him about the first anonymous letter and about the police and about the birdwatcher saving me from getting an ASBO for being a vandal. I can't believe I didn't tell him about it last night but then we rushed off to the Hanford Colosseum straight after he turned up and on the way back I was too busy telling them what had happened.

'Oh,' he says when I've finished.

I expected a bit more than that. I thought that the whole police thing was a fairly exciting story. Still I've got to remember that he plays a lot of chess and that probably weakens your ability to get excited after a while.

'Anyway I've had another one,' And I tell him what it says and the different things that I think it might mean. 'What do you think I should do? Should I go to the park?'

'I think you should...'

And then he stops. He's not looking at me any more. He's looking behind me. I turn round. Standing right there is Katie Pierce.

'Hello, boys,' she says.

'What do you want Katie?'

She smiles.

'I just came over to see if you've got any issues you'd like me to raise at school council next week.'

'You're not our class representative,' I say. 'We voted for Emma Roberts.'

'I know,' says Katie. 'But after the vote I explained to Emma what a stressful job being a class representative is and how many friends you might lose and how if you don't put people's points of view forward in the proper way they might be tempted to find you in the toilets and give you a good slapping. And Emma decided that perhaps she wasn't quite ready to represent the class and that maybe I should do it for her. And you know how shy I am but I decided that if it would help Emma and it would help the class then I would sacrifice my own feelings for the good of others and do it.'

'You're such a good person, Katie,' I tell her sarcastically.

'You'll make me blush, Mickey. Maybe I'll go as red as you do when you talk to a girl you fancy.'

She's got me there. I do go red sometimes when I talk to girls I fancy. I can't help it. Even thinking about it makes me start to go...oh no.

'Mickey, you're going red now,' observes Katie. 'Does that mean that you fancy me?'

'No,' I say.

'You would say that, wouldn't you?' says Katie. 'But I think we all know the truth. What can I say, Mickey? I just don't think about you in that way.'

'I don't want you to...'

'You'll just have to accept it, Mickey. Nothing like that can ever happen between us.'

'I just said that...'

'But I want you to know that we can always be friends.'

'Friends? I don't...'

'And, as your friend, let me give you a piece of advice. Year 9 girls, and I think I can speak for all of them here, are going to turn you down if you ask them out. You're just not their type. Any of them. Maybe you should consider looking for a girlfriend in Year 8 or Year 7. They aren't quite as sophisticated as we are. And if that doesn't work you could always try girls in Primary schools. You'd just have to be prepared to play with their Barbies now and then.'

'Katie...'

'Don't thank me. I'm just trying to help. I see it as part of my role as class representative.'

'But...'

'You know Mickey, you're still very red. You must really fancy me a lot.'

And she turns round and walks off before I can say anything else. I feel like a football team who's just been beaten 10 – 0.

'You are quite red, you know,' says Umair.

'Shut up!' I tell him. 'You were about to tell me what you thought I should do about this note thing.'

The pips go for the start of first lesson. Umair frowns.

'I don't know why you're asking me,' he says. 'I

don't know anything about it. Do what you want. I've got to get to Maths.'

He grabs his bag, stands up and rushes off.

I don't know what got him so angry all of a sudden. I thought he liked Maths.

I spend the next five lessons deciding whether to go or not. It's good to have something to distract me or I might have had to learn something. By the time the bell goes for lunch I've made up my mind and by 12.40 I'm at the lake as instructed. But I don't stay there. Instead I hide myself in some nearby bushes and I watch. And what a surprise – at 12.45 a police car speeds into the park and screeches to a halt by the lake. Two policemen get out and start looking all around for something or someone and I've got a good idea who that person might be.

After five minutes they get back in their car and drive off. I wait a bit longer and then get out of the bushes and head back to school.

Something very strange is going on.

CHAPTER 17

I go straight home after school. I figure that to solve this case I'm going to need a very good idea very soon. And the only way I know to get a good idea is to put my feet up in my office and keep eating crisps and swigging coke until one comes. Either that or I get the hiccups so badly that I forget I need an idea at all.

As soon as I see her I get the feeling that there's going to be trouble. You can sometimes tell how people are feeling just from the way they stand and from the way that Jenni is standing outside my shed she isn't very happy. I'm not in the mood for another argument so I decide to back off and come back when she's gone but she turns round and spots me just before I can disappear. I've no option but to go over to the shed.

'Were you going to run off?' she says when I get there.

'What?' I say. 'I don't know what you're talking about.'

'You were going to run off as soon as you saw me,' she says following me into the shed. 'Is that because you haven't got anywhere with the case?'

'No,' I say.

'My brother says you spent most of yesterday in a bin. I don't see how that's getting the job done.'

I was hoping that he hadn't mentioned last night to her.

'Your brother doesn't understand the finer points of detective work,' I tell her. If in doubt, bluff it out.

'My brother might not be no genius but even he can see that someone who can just about manage to find an empty pizza box is going to really struggle when it comes to finding a real live human being.'

It looks like DJ Smarty has really gone into details. And the more details he's gone into then the worse I'm going to look. I don't even bother to answer her this time because she'll probably have another juicy example of my stupidity provided by her brother ready to throw at me. I wonder if it's bullying to hit a kid three years younger than you when you've got a good reason.

'I should sack you,' says Jenni. 'You don't have the faintest idea what you're doing. You spend your time making a fool of yourself and I'm embarrassed for people to know that I ever talked to you.'

I don't think I'll be asking her for a reference.

'But...' she says and then she stops.

'But...' I repeat to make sure she's said it.

'But I can't,' she finishes.

'Why not?' I say and then straight away realise that maybe I shouldn't have. It sounds like I can't think of a good reason why she shouldn't sack me.

'I can't do it because I'm too busy with rehearsals and because we've got even less time than we had before and because I don't know anybody else who will do it instead.'

'Not because you think that even though I've made a couple of mistakes that basically I'm still a good detective and you have faith that when the chips are down I'll come through for you?' I suggest.

'No,' she confirms.

'Just checking.' I remember something that she said a second ago. 'What do you mean about us having less time?'

She shrugs.

'The record company have bumped us. Some chart band want the studio on Saturday so we've got to do our demo on Friday night.'

'That means you need Desiree by tomorrow.'

'You worked that all out by yourself,' she says. 'We need her at the recording studio by 8 o'clock tomorrow. If you haven't got her by then I don't ever want to see your face again.'

I try to nod like I believe I can do it. But I don't think I've got a chance.

'I won't hold my breath,' she says.

'Don't,' I say. 'It doesn't help you when you're singing.'

'I don't sing,' she hisses. 'I rap.'

And with that she stomps out of my shed and slams the door behind her. There's something about the door of my shed which seems to make everyone who comes into it want to slam it. It can't be long before it falls off.

I know I should sit straight down to try and think of a way to solve the case now I've got even less time but I can't be bothered. The whole thing is hopeless. And being on my own in the shed reminds me how hopeless and depressing it is so I decide to go inside instead. Someone might tell me off which would distract me from thinking about what a great big failure I'm going to be at 8 o'clock tomorrow night.

My mum's cooking in the kitchen.

'What's for tea?' I ask her.

'Hello Mickey,' she says.

'Oh, yeah. Hello Mum. What's for tea?'

'Did you have a nice day?'

'No. What's for tea?'

'I had quite a successful day, Mickey. I may even have saved someone's life today.'

'Good. What's for tea?'

'They had an internal haemorrhage and I got to them just in time.'

'Oh right...What's...'

'And you will have an internal haemorrhage if you ask me once more what's for tea. I am not simply your cook. I am not simply your mother. I am a person in my own right and I saved someone's life today and nobody seems to care. Your sister is on the phone, your father is watching some rubbish about killer bees on the television and you are obsessed with what's for tea even though I bet that not five minutes ago you were stuffing your face full of cheese'n'onion crisps and spoiling your appetite.'

'It was salt'n'vinegar...'

'I don't care what it was. What I care about is that I saved someone's life today. I did a good thing. And nobody's noticed.'

My mum gets in these moods sometimes. Normally after she's been drinking wine. Then she either hugs me too much or cries and says she wishes she'd gone backpacking round the world when she was twenty one and not got herself stuck with a marriage and two children.

'I bet the person whose life you saved has noticed,' I tell her.

'Of course they've noticed,' she snaps. 'And do you know what they're doing about it?'

'Buying you flowers.'

'No. They're making a formal complaint and they're suing.'

'Why?'

'Because I pressed too hard when I was trying to staunch the flow of blood and I made a small bruise.'

'Oh.'

'They might even report me to the police for assault.'

'You might be in the same cell as I was. I'd have to come and get you out,' I tell her but I guess from the look on her face that she isn't into laughing about the ironic twists of fate.

'You're not helping, Mickey,' she tells me.

'I still don't know what's for tea,' I remind her to get her mind off the idea of being sued and put in prison because she bothered to save some ungrateful guy's life.

'Will you shut up about your tea or you will find that the only way you can enjoy it is through an intravenous drip.'

I can't help feeling that some of the medical dramas that my mum watches on Channel 4 are having a bad effect on her.

'Now get out of here,' she says.

I might as well. I think I've been all the help I can here.

'Oh. Before you do. Find me the radio and put it on. I feel like listening to something moronic – it will put me in the right frame of mind for the conversation round the tea table.'

She really is having a bad day.

I go through to the lounge where my dad is watching his nature programme and grab the portable radio and bring it back through to the kitchen. I set it to the local music station. It normally plays the kind of rubbish that my mum likes.

I'm right too. The first song that's playing is Girl Power's single. My mum starts singing along even though she doesn't even know it. That shows you how bad the song is. It's so predictable. So like every other lousy girl band song you've ever heard that you can sing it without ever having heard it properly before. And just to make it even more annoying they sing the chorus about a hundred times before the song finally finishes.

'That's a request for Luke Gray,' The DJ's voice comes over the chorus as it fades out. 'Luke's working in the abattoir in East Street at the moment and he wants his girlfriend to know that he still loves her even if she insists on becoming a vegetarian. And to show he loves her, he's going to try really hard this week not to bring home any blood covered knives. Warms the cockles of your heart, doesn't it?'

It doesn't warm the cockles of my heart. I decide to head up to my room.

'You're listening to Johnny Feegan on Bubble FM. And, now to the competition I mentioned before. We're giving away two tickets to tomorrow's concert by Girl Power plus an opportunity to meet up with the band beforehand and just hang out and chill with them for an hour before the gig.'

I change my mind about heading up to my room.

'All you've got to do is answer this question. Now it's a fairly tough question as it's such a good prize but I'm sure someone out there will be a big enough fan of the girls to find out the answer.'

'Mickey,' says my mum. 'I thought I told you I wanted music.'

'Mum,' I tell her. 'Will you be quiet? This is important.'

'The question is,' says the DJ, 'where would you find the world's largest concentration of killer bees?'

I don't know.

Bang. My mum cracks me round the head with a soup ladle.

'Ow. What was that for?'

'That was for telling me to be quiet.'

'Ring 000 999 888 777 if you know the answer and always get permission from the person who pays the bill. Or at least make sure they're out. We'll announce the winner at 8 o'clock tomorrow morning.'

I don't know whether it was the crack on the head with the ladle but something has reminded me about what my mum said a couple of minutes ago. My dad. A nature documentary. Killer bees.

'Dad!' I shout and head for the lounge.

'It's no use going whining to your father,' my mum shouts after me. 'He thinks I should hit you with the kitchen utensils more often.'

CHAPTER 18

Mexico. That's the answer. It took some getting out of my dad because first I had to agree with him that he was right and that the things they taught you on nature programmes were useful and that I will watch more of them in future. And then I had to listen to a lecture about how these crazy scientists took loads of normal bees and then mated them with each other until they became mad killer bees and then one of the scientists forgot to close a window or something and so the killer bees all escaped and got out into Mexico where they spend loads of time stinging people and hardly any making honey or doing dances to tell the other bees where the pollen is. They sound like a bee version of the morons at the back.

So I've got the answer and, after I accidentally trip up on the phone cable to rip it out of its socket, my sister's phone call comes to a sudden end and I'm able to phone the radio station. The woman who answers sounds really surprised when I say Mexico. I bet that's because the DJ made the question deliberately hard so that nobody would win and then he could give the prize to his kid.

But his plans are ruined and mine are about to take a giant leap forward. It's the next morning and it's 7.58 AM and I'm already at breakfast which surprises my mum.

'What are you up to?' she says when she sees me.

'Nothing,' I say. 'I just wanted to see whether I won the competition.'

But the truth is that I know I have. Normally I don't believe in superstitions and fate and star signs but there's something about the way everything fitted into place yesterday that tells me that I'm destined to win those tickets. My dad could have been watching a documentary about any creature at all but it turned out to be killer bees and my mum might not have had such a bad day at work that she wanted to listen to the radio and then I would never have known about the competition.

But it all fell into place. And it fell into place for a reason. To give me a chance to solve the case.

'You are just the saddest person, trying to win tickets to a Girl Power concert,' says Karen who's diluting the skimmed milk on her muesli with water so it's got even fewer calories.

The one drawback of the whole destiny situation is that Karen keeps having a go at me because Girl

Power are such a terrible group. She's right as well which makes it worse but I can't let her know that.

'It's better than liking groups like Detritus and Pondweed,' I shoot back. 'They don't even wash.'

'That's just prejudice,' says Karen. 'It's only Scumbag out of Detritus who doesn't wash and he doesn't wash to make a statement about the importance of living organically in an era when global corporations are creating mass paranoia about people's natural smells in order to sell them overpriced aerosols which mask humanity's natural musk and destroy the ozone layer at the same time resulting in global warming and the ice caps melting and floods and the extinction of the human race.'

My mum and me both stare at Karen.

'Where did you get that from?' says my mum.

'He said it at that press conference that was on the news last night.'

'I remember,' says my mum. 'Wasn't he wearing a Nike top when he was going on about the evil of global corporations?'

'Yeah,' nods Karen.

'Aren't they a global corporation?' asks my mum.

'Yeah,' says Karen, 'but their stuff is cool.'

'OK everybody,' says the DJ on the radio, 'It's time to find out who has won yesterday's incredible prize of a meeting with Girl Power and front row seats at their concert.'

'Ssh,' I say to my mum and Karen.

'To remind you,' says the DJ, 'The question was about killer bees and the answer is...I'm pausing to build up the tension here...Are you feeling tense out there?'

'No,' says Karen.

'Shut up,' I tell her.

'The answer was,' says the DJ, 'Mexico.'

'Yes,' I say.

'Sad boy,' observes Karen.

'Now,' says the DJ, 'We didn't have very many correct answers at all because it was such a difficult question so I don't even need a hat to pick out the name of the winner.'

I bet they only had one correct answer.

'So without further ado...Come to think of it where does the word 'ado' come from...If you know why don't you phone up or email in and tell us or if you've had a an amusing experience in which the word "ado" was used or if you've ever been to a do and thought that it was more of a don't then phone or email or even fax in and we'll tell your story live on the radio.'

'Come on,' I shout at the radio.

'What was I doing?' says the DJ.

'Being a moron,' I tell him.

'Oh yeah...The competition...Without further ado...don't forget to ring in now...the winner is...'

Mickey Sharp, Mickey Sharp, Mickey Sharp.

'George Martin.'

What?

I've lost. I can't believe it. How can I have lost? It was my destiny to win.

'It says here that George is a thirteen year old boy who lives at 17 Abbey Road, Hanford. Just be at the station at five o'clock, George, and we'll take you down to the Hanford Colosseum and introduce you to the girls. You'll be having your own private meeting with five gorgeous pop stars. And all courtesy of Bubble FM the station which lifts you into the air.'

Who is this George Martin kid anyway and what does he think he's doing knowing about killer bees? He's probably some sad specimen who spends his evenings reading encyclopaedias. He's ruined my last chance of solving the case.

'Never mind, Mickey,' says Karen. 'There'll be another totally manufactured, talentless girl band that nobody's ever heard of in the charts next week. Maybe you'll win a competition to go and see them.'

Even though it's early I decide that I've got no option but to go to school.

CHAPTER 19

When I get to the front door there's another letter. Exactly the same as before. This time I know I'm not going to trust it. I'm going to put it straight into the bin without even opening it because it's bound to be another trap. But I can't put it in a bin until I actually find one so I stick it in my pocket until then. I get my bike and ride to school. It's raining again which matches my mood.

There's still about twenty minutes to go before school starts when I get there so there's hardly anybody about. And because it's Friday even the teachers' car park is empty. Some teachers try to get to school early at the start of the week but by Friday they've given up and they charge in at the last minute just like the kids.

When you're this early there's never anybody about to stop you going inside so I head up to our form room to lean against my favourite radiator. Even the Thick Girl with Glasses and the Even Thicker Girl with Pigtails aren't in early today.

I notice a chunky coin under a desk. I'm not rich enough to turn down the chance of free money so I pull the chair out and bend down. I can't reach it but it's definitely a two pound coin. Since nobody's around I get on my hands and knees and crawl under the desk.

Just as my fingers touch it I hear the voices.

'You've got to tell me now.'

'I don't have to tell you anything.'

A boy and a girl.

'I've done what you said. Now you've got to give me an answer.'

'I'm not ready yet.'

Umair and Katie Pierce.

'Come on, Katie. I'm desperate. I can't concentrate on my work any more. It's like you've put a spell on me. All I can think about is what you're going to say.'

'I'm really upset for you.'

'When will you be able to tell me?'

Tell him what?

'When I decide.'

That's not much help.

'Katie, I've done everything you want. Every single thing. Put me out of my misery. Say yes.'

'Umair, you should know a girl likes to play hard to get.'

'This isn't a game, Katie.'

'Everything's a game, Umair. Not just chess. Love.

Hate. All that stuff. It's all a game. You might as well enjoy it.'

'But I can't enjoy it, Katie. Not until you say yes.'

'You're getting boring, Umair.'

'But Katie...'

'And you know how I hate being bored.'

'Katie...'

I hear a bang. I think Katie's walked out. Has Umair followed her? I twist my head round. I can see a pair of legs so I figure that he hasn't. The legs walk over to the set of desks I'm hiding under and pull out a chair. Umair sits down.

This is not an easy position to be in. Either physically or mentally. Physically, I'm kind of cramped and there's a big chance that I might get Umair's shoe planted accidentally in my face at any moment. Mentally, I'm having to come to terms with what I've just heard. Which is what? As far as I can tell it all points to one thing. Umair has fallen for Katie Pierce big time and was asking her out. Umair was asking Katie Pierce out! I have to think it twice to even start getting my head round it. Umair, who was my best mate since primary school. Umair, who's the only person I know who might hate Katie Pierce more than me. And he was begging her to give him a chance.

'No!'

There's big bang on the desk above me. Umair must

have smashed his fist into it because he's so angry. Or maybe even his head.

'No!'

This time he stamps his foot. Right on my hand.

'Ow!'

'What the…who's under there?'

I scramble out.

'Hi,' I say trying to sound casual.

'What are you doing?'

'Er…There was a two pound coin under the desk.'

'How long have you been there?'

'Hard to say really.'

He's got a photo in his hand that he was looking at when I popped up. I can't see what it is. But I can guess. He really is under Katie's spell.

He stuffs it away in his pocket.

'What's that?' I say.

'Nothing.'

This is silly. I can't pretend that I haven't heard. He knows that I was either here all the time or that I can materialise anywhere at any time and I don't think he takes Star Trek that seriously.

'I can guess what the photo is,' I say.

'I don't believe you,' he says.

'I was under the table, remember. I heard you talking to Katie.'

'That doesn't mean that you know what the photo is.'

He's really making this difficult for both of us. I

would have thought he'd do his best to shrug it off but instead he's dragging out all the nasty details. And all the nasty details are going to make him squirm – not me, so I can't really understand why he's doing it.

'Don't make me say it,' I tell him.

'I want you to say it,' he fires back.

I haven't got any choice. Bang goes a beautiful friendship.

'It's Katie Pierce.'

'WHAT?'

'It's Katie Pierce.'

'DON'T BE STUPID.'

Umair really should learn to quit when things are going badly because in this situation they can only get worse.

'Look, I heard you talking to her,' I tell him. 'You were begging her to give you an answer. You were saying that you couldn't concentrate on your work anymore. She was talking about love being a game and playing hard to get. You were asking her out and you've managed to get hold of some photo of her to look at because you're so into her.'

'You think I was asking Katie Pierce out? You think I was looking at a picture of her?'

He sounds really angry with me but it's not my fault. I nod. There's nothing else to say.

'Really, Mr Detective. Maybe this will change your mind.'

He pulls the photograph out of his pocket and slams it down on the table.

It's a photo of a red book. That's all. Nothing but a red book.

'That look like Katie to you?'

'Er…Well…Maybe not.'

'So don't ever say anything again about me fancying Katie Pierce or asking her out, all right?'

He's really angry.

'Okay, okay,' I tell him.

He calms down a little bit. I know I should leave him to calm down more but I can't. I want to know too much.

'Why are you looking at a really boring picture and smashing the desk to bits at the same time?'

He's on the point of flaring right up again. But he stops himself

'It's nothing.'

'It's got to be something,' I tell him.

He doesn't say anything. It takes a real effort but I don't either. I figure give him some space and then maybe…

'It's my diary, Okay?'

'Your diary?'

He nods.

'She's got it and she won't give it back.'

I don't understand why this is such a big deal.

'No disrespect to your hobbies,' I tell him, 'But

losing the dates of your next chess match can't be that important.'

His head slumps onto the desk like he can't look at me.

'It's not that kind of diary.'

'You mean…' Suddenly I can't look at him either. '…feelings and stuff.'

'Worse.'

'Worse than feelings?'

'Poetry.'

It is worse. Much worse

'You've been writing poetry?'

'Nobody was supposed to know.'

'But I thought you liked chess.'

'You can like chess and poetry, you know.'

Umair's one unlucky boy. Liking chess is bad enough. But poetry too. There should be a law or something.

At least he's got his head up off the table.

'She said she'd show everybody in the whole year if I don't do what she wants,' he said.

I wince for him. If Katie Pierce's decides Year 9 is going to hear something then you can be sure they are. And if it's your soppy poetry then your reputation is gone in a second. And once your reputation is gone then the bullies start coming for you. They're like sharks.

'You've got to get it back.'

'I know that,' he snaps. 'But how? I don't know where it is. She's not stupid. She gave me a photo as proof that she's got it but I've not seen the real thing for a week.'

'What were you doing bringing it into school?' I ask him.

It's a good question. If I ever find myself writing soppy poetry it's staying locked up in my bedroom.

'It had my chess openings in the back,' he admits. 'And I needed to learn a complex line in the Ruy Lopez.'

I'm not letting him off that easy.

'So if you've got to bring it in to school you don't let it out of your sight, right?'

'I kept it in my bag.'

'So how did she get it?'

'She sits behind me in Maths,' he explains, 'and there was this really interesting simultaneous equation. I got distracted working it out and when I looked up from my textbook it had gone.'

Maths, chess and poetry. Together they're a lethal combination. But he's too depressed already for me to point this out.

'She said she'd give it back to me,' he says, 'If I just did something for her. But I did it and she's still holding out.'

I can't believe Umair's fallen for that. There must be some really dodgy rhymes in that diary.

'You know you can't trust Katie Pierce,' I say. 'The only way you're going to get that diary back is to get something on her so you can deal.'

'Like what?'

'I don't know.'

I sit there thinking for a second. And then something else pops into my mind. 'Hey. One thing I don't get. Why was she blackmailing you? What did she want you to do?'

Umair looks down at the table.

'Not much,' he mumbles.

'Katie Pierce isn't going to go to all that trouble for not much,' I tell him. 'What was it?'

'Well...er...um...you see...it was...I didn't want to... no choice,' says Umair, which makes about as much sense as the past tense in French.

'What?' I say.

Umair looks up.

'It was you.'

'Me?'

He nods.

'What have I got to do with anything? What did she want with me?'

'Revenge.'

It hits me hard even though I'd always known it was coming. Katie isn't one to forgive and forget but somehow she still took me by surprise. But using my best friend against me. That's hard. I tell myself again – you don't cross Katie Pierce and not expect some comeback. And I'd crossed her a few times this year. Like getting her caught smoking by her mum and making sure she had to keep coaching an under eleven football team and nearly ruining her chances to be Head Girl. I did all those things but I only did them because I was trying to solve cases and she got in the way. Which isn't to say that I didn't enjoy them.

'She came up with this whole plan to get back at me?'

Now the shock's wearing off there's something about that which makes me feel quite proud. Nobody normally puts that much effort into anything to do with me.

'Yeah,' nods Umair.

But the smug feeling fades as I realise what this means.

'You went along with it?'

Umair looks a bit ashamed.

'That's why you were interested in the case?'

Umair looks more ashamed.

'We used to be best mates,' I say. 'Just because we're not any more doesn't give you the right to start siding with Katie Pierce.'

'I wasn't siding with her,' says Umair. 'I was trying to get my diary back. I didn't know Katie was going to go that far. I thought she was just going to throw gunge over you or something.'

'What do you mean "that far?"' I say. 'Do you mean

she's already had her revenge? Well, if she has it's pretty rubbish revenge because I haven't even noticed.'

Unless...

'It's not getting my dad to make us watch nature documentaries all the time, is it?'

Umair shakes his head.

'It's the letters.'

'The letters?'

And bang it all fits into place. That's why she needed Umair to find out about the case. So that she could put the details in her letters which would tempt me to come to the places she wanted me to.

'Thanks to you I was arrested,' I tell Umair. 'I might still be in jail now if it hadn't been for some birdwatcher.'

'She didn't tell me she was going to do that,' protests Umair. 'I didn't think she was that bad. I was going to try and give you a hint in registration yesterday when you asked me if I thought you should go to the lake but she came over just as I was about to say something.'

That explains why he suddenly got so angry. He was feeling guilty because he knew the letter was a trap.

'There's this one...kind of...love poem,' he says quietly. 'It's got someone's name in it.'

I have to admit Katie had him in a tough spot. Like he said he didn't know she was going to go that far and if the poem actually said a girl's name.

'And I used a really bad rhyme for kiss.'

I grin even though what he said wasn't that funny. But it's not so tense any more. I'm not sure we're friends again but I don't think we're going to have to hit each other.

'Hey,' I suddenly remember. 'I got another anonymous letter this morning.'

I pull it out of my pocket and rip it open. It says :

YOUR LAST CHANCE TO SOLVE THIS CASE AND GET DESIREE BACK TO THE REALLY TOUGH CREW IS TO BE IN THE GRAVEYARD AT 100 TODAY.

I read it twice. A pounding starts inside my skull. It's either the beginning of a headache or the start of a plan.

CHAPTER 20

We're not at the graveyard at one o'clock. We're there at twelve. We have to bunk out of French to get there that early and Umair has never bunked a lesson before so I had to persuade him.

'I'm still not sure about this,' he says. 'Something is bound to go wrong.'

'Things have already gone wrong,' I tell him. 'I've been arrested and you're being blackmailed. What we're going to do today is put things right.'

I don't wait for any more arguments.

'Come on,' I say, 'and keep away from any walls with graffiti on or any lakes.'

We walk into the graveyard. Just walking in there seems to make everything quieter. The next time I open my mouth I realise that I'm whispering.

'We need somewhere where we can hide but see everything.'

'Up there,' suggests Umair.

He indicates a little bit of a hill. We head up there. He's right. From here we can see it all.

'We need to get out of sight,' I say. 'You get down behind that stone and I'll go behind this one.'

We check around. There's nobody about. We both get down. And start waiting. We're right at the top of the graveyard so the only way we're going to be spotted is if someone actually visits the graves we're hiding behind. I check mine out. The guy in my grave died in 1956 so I don't suppose he'll be getting many visitors.

'Hey,' I whisper to Umair. 'When did yours die?'

'1975.'

That's good. I don't think that anyone's going to visit that one either. I don't see the point in visiting graves. If I was dead I wouldn't want people coming out to visit my grave. I'd rather they went and visited my shed. At least that's somewhere that I hung out. They could go and sit in my shed and eat a packet of crisps. That would be a much better way of remembering me than coming out to a field and looking at a stone.

'Hey,' whispers Umair.

'What?'

'There she is.'

I take a peek around the side of my gravestone. Katie Pierce has just come into the graveyard with some boy who's carrying a big black bin bag. They start walking up the hill towards us. I realise that I'm holding my breath.

They keep coming our way.

Please stop, I say inside my head.

But they keep coming. Further and further up the hill.

They're so close now that I can't risk looking anymore. I signal to Umair and he pulls his head back too.

'I can't carry this any further, Katie. I'm knackered,' the boy tells Katie

'And I thought you were a big man and not a little boy,' she answers. 'I suppose here will have to do.'

'I still don't understand why you've made me carry this bag all this way.'

'Your job isn't to understand,' Katie tells him. 'Your job is to lift things. Empty out the bag.'

'I've been wondering what's in here.'

He's not the only one.

'Now's your chance to find out.'

'You haven't murdered anyone, have you, Katie?'

It's good to know that Katie's friends think she's mad too.

'No,' says Katie. 'Just tip out the bag and stop asking so many questions.'

I can't resist looking even if it does mean there's a chance she'll spot me. The boy lifts it up and turns it over. A whole load of black soil comes pouring out.

'What's that for?' says the boy.

'I told you to stop asking so many questions.'

'Yeah, but this is getting really weird.'

'Just go down and get the shovel.'

'Katie,' says the boy. 'You know that I like you and everything but this is too weird for me. I don't think I can help you any more.'

'Don't be pathetic. Just go and get the shovel and then you're finished and I might even let you kiss me.'

'Hold on, Katie,' says the boy. 'I wouldn't be up for that. I'm the best kisser in Year 9 but I couldn't get it right in a graveyard. It would interfere with my concentration and mess up my technique.'

'All right,' says Katie. 'Just get the shovel and we'll go somewhere else.'

'Sorry, Katie. This is really beginning to freak me out. I'm getting out of here.'

'One thing before you go.'

'What?'

'You aren't the best kisser in Year 9. Trust me. I've kissed most of the boys so I should know.'

'But I know that I'm...'

'You know nothing,' Katie tells him. 'It's like kissing a washing machine. Now get out of here if you're going.'

The boy doesn't say anything else. He just turns and runs off down the hill and out of the graveyard.

Katie watches him go. She shakes her head.

'Boys,' she says to herself. 'Absolutely useless. I'll have to get it myself.'

She walks off down the hill.

'Psst,' says Umair.

'What?'

'Don't you see what she's doing?'

'She's ruining that guy's ego,' I answer. 'He'll probably be practising kissing on his pillow for the next month.'

'Not that,' says Umair. 'With the soil and the shovel.'

I think about it for a second.

'No.'

'It's just like what she did to you the first time with the half-finished graffiti and the spray can on the ground. She left the evidence and then phoned the police and they saw the clues and decided you must be guilty and arrested you.'

I still don't get it.

'This time the evidence is a shovel and a big heap of soil.'

'So?' I say.

She's going to ring the police and tell them that someone of your description is digging up graves. They'll turn up here see the shovel and the earth and you'll be under arrest again.'

I can't believe it.

'She wouldn't do that,' I say. 'I mean even Katie has got limits.'

'Has she?' said Umair. 'She would have ruined my reputation and I hadn't done anything to her for years. Think what she'd be happy to do to you. We should get out of here fast.'

I shake my head. I'm getting an idea. We need a bit of luck but it might just work.

'I think we can get Katie Pierce off your back,' I tell him.

'How?'

'There's no time to explain. Chuck me your mobile phone.'

He doesn't look too sure.

'Now, before she gets back.'

He throws it over. I switch it on and press nine three times.

'Hello emergency services. Which service do you require?'

'Police.'

'What's your name, sir?'

'John Walton.'

That's actually the name of the Head of my school.

'What do you wish to report?'

'I'm in Hanford Cemetery and there's a teenage girl digging up dead bodies.'

'I beg your pardon?'

'I'm in Hanford Cemetery and there's a teenage girl with long dark hair in a Hanford High Uniform digging up dead bodies.'

'Is this a hoax?'

'No. We need a police car down here now or else she could soon be breaking into coffins.'

'You're sure she isn't burying someone?'

'No, she's digging someone up.'

'I imagine the two things must look very similar.'

'It doesn't matter. She's in a school uniform. She shouldn't be digging up graves.'

'There's probably a reasonable explanation.'

'She's still digging.'

'She could be on work experience.'

'I want the police to come.'

'We're undermanned.'

'She's underground.'

'Oh all right. We'll get a car along as soon as we can.'

I click off the phone and look across at Umair. He puts his finger to his lips. I take a peek round the gravestone. Katie Pierce is coming up the hill carrying a shovel. I hope that the police aren't going to be long. My watch says it's 12.33.

Katie reaches the pile of dirt and sticks the shovel into it. She picks up the big black bin bag and scrunches it up in her hand till it's as small as she can make it.

My watch says 12.35.

Katie starts looking round her. I realise that she's looking for somewhere to hide so that she can wait for me to arrive and get caught. And the best place for her to hide is behind the big gravestone where I am.

My watch says 12.37.

Katie starts to walk up towards the gravestone that I'm hiding behind.

I'm too nervous to look at my watch.

I hear a siren. Katie hears it too. She stops for a moment and listens. Then she shrugs and starts walking again. The siren gets nearer. She stops again. There's a tiny bit of doubt on her face. But it's only a tiny bit of doubt and it's got a great big wodge of arrogance to overcome. It doesn't succeed. Katie thinks she's so perfect that it would never occur to her that her plan could be going wrong. She fiddles in her pocket for her mobile phone and then carries on walking towards me. She's so near now that I have to take the precautionary step of stopping breathing. I hope it's only going to be a temporary measure.

She's less than five metres away when the squeal of brakes makes her turn round. A police car stops just outside the gates. A policewoman get out of the car and rushes into the cemetery. She spots Katie and heads straight for her.

I'd love her to run. I'd love to see Katie chased right through the cemetery, jumping over gravestones and diving for cover behind marble angels. But that isn't going to happen. Katie doesn't lose her cool that easily. She stands and waits until the policewoman gets to her.

'Would you care to explain the shovel and the soil?' asks the policewoman.

'I don't know what you're talking about,' says Katie. 'I'm here to pay my respects to a very dear relation of mine. She hasn't died, she's just gone into another room.'

There are times when I almost admire Katie Pierce.

'What's her name?' demands the policewoman suspiciously.

'Er…,' says Katie, trying frantically to read the nearest gravestone. 'Mary Shelley. Her memory is so tender I can barely bring myself to say her name.'

'You must be very sensitive,' says the policewoman.

'I am,' sniffles Katie.

'Being so upset about someone who died in 1789.'

'Oh,' says Katie.

'You'd better come down to the station with me,' says the policewoman. 'This is going to take some sorting out.'

She leads Katie off down the hill.

'I can't believe that worked,' says Umair as we watch the police car drive off.

I find his attitude a bit disappointing. I hoped he'd have more faith in my plan.

'What do you think will happen to her?'

Already I can hear the worry in Umair's voice. You see the problem is that he's basically a good guy. But he's caught up in a bad situation. And when you're taking on girls like Katie Pierce you can't afford to be good. You've got to be ruthless.

'She'll be fine,' I say.

'Do you think they'll put her in jail?'

'We'll never be that lucky.'

'I don't know about this.'

'Katie will be fine. She always is. But she was quite happy to have me get into loads of trouble. Let's leave her for a bit.'

'I don't know.'

'We'll deal with Katie soon,' I reassure him. 'And we'll get your diary back. But now I've got to get back to the case.'

'Oh yeah,' he says trying to sound interested when you can tell he's really not. 'What's going on with that?'

Even though I know he's not that bothered I tell him anyway. About how there was this competition on the radio and about how I was sure I was going to win and that if I had that would have given me a really good chance to solve the case. And then when everything was sorted out what blows the whole thing apart is that some kid called George Martin wins it and so now I'm stuck with this case which I've got to solve within six hours and I haven't got the faintest idea how I'm going to do it.

'That's tough,' says Umair when I've finished. 'Let's

get back to school. I'm going to have a double portion of chips.'

Some use he is. I'm well on the way to getting his diary back and all he can think about is chips. Still it reminds me I'm quite hungry. So now we're both thinking about chips. I'm no use either.

CHAPTER 21

'*My what big eyes you've got grandma all the better to see you with my dear my what big ears you've got all the better to hear you my dear my what beautiful teeth you've got all the better...*'

'Stop,' shouts Miss Hurley.

'What?' I ask.

'Mickey, this is the dramatic conclusion to the story, and you are reading it without any expression so it sounds as dull as dishwater and without any pauses so it doesn't make any sense.'

'I didn't want to read, did I?' I say.

It's true. I didn't. I hate reading out loud in class. There's always a chance that my voice is going to pull its trick of starting to squeak and, even if that doesn't happen, you can be sure that as soon as you start the morons at the back will start throwing things at you. It's dead easy for English teachers to go on about how you should read like they do with lots of expression but they don't have rubbers bouncing off their heads all the time.

'Reading is not a choice, Mickey,' says Miss Hurley. 'Reading is a necessity.'

Miss Hurley hates it when people say they don't want to read. She thinks that reading is the most important thing in the world. But I'm not stopping her thinking that. I just wish she'd leave me alone to think about my case. That happens to be the thing I think is most important at the moment. That's the problem with teachers. They never seem to understand that just because they think that reading or equations or crop rotation in the Middle Ages is really wonderful not everybody else is going to. They keep going on about this stuff even when it's really obvious that everybody's bored and then they tell you off for not trying. Just once I'd like to see teachers be made to do things by kids and see how they like it. I'd love to see Miss Hurley be told that she was in detention if she couldn't send a text message to Mr Walton or that she'd be put on report if she didn't get to the end of Level Two of Halo 3 by the time the bell went.

'Now finish off reading your paragraph. And try and do it with some expression.'

'*All the better to eat you with*,' I say.

'Thank you,' says Miss Hurley. 'Those seven words were better.'

'Can I have a credit, Miss?' I ask.

It's the last lesson of Friday and my last chance to reach my credit target.

'Of course you can't, Mickey,' says Miss Hurley.

Looks like I've missed it then.

'Now then,' continues Miss Hurley, 'When we first read this book as children we were no doubt so terrified as to what the wolf might do to Little Red Riding Hood that we didn't think too much about the credibility of the story. But now as more mature fourteen-year-old readers we must ask different questions. Is it really believable that just because the wolf says that he is Red Riding Hood's grandmother she would believe him? We can assume that Little Red Riding Hood did not have particular difficulties with her eyesight. How could she fail to distinguish between an old lady and a wild beast?'

Miss Hurley's obviously never met my grandmother.

'It is ludicrous,' says Miss Hurley. 'One character in a story claims to be another and simply gets away with it. We must treat such a tale with great caution.'

I don't know why Miss Hurley thinks she needs to prove that Little Red Riding Hood is a dodgy story. I knew that from the title. Never trust a story where the main character is named after her coat.

'But in children's literature,' says Miss Hurley with a sigh, 'Such incredible plots are commonplace. Many writers seem to believe that they can get away with anything when it comes to younger readers. However, the story...'

The pips go for the end of the day. There is no teacher in the world who can stop our class packing up the moment they know the last lesson of the week has finished and at least Miss Hurley isn't dumb enough to try.

'We'll finish our discussion next week,' she says. 'Have a good weekend everyone.'

Everybody starts to rush out of the classroom. Everybody except me. Something Miss Hurley says has just hit me right smack bang in the face.

'What's the matter Mickey?'

'Nothing, Miss. I was just thinking about something you said.'

'Really?'

She sounds very surprised.

'Yes, Miss. About how Little Red Riding Hood is a rubbish story because nobody would ever mistake their granny for a wolf.'

'I didn't exactly say it was rubbish,' she says. 'But I take your point.'

'But, Miss, even though that's true it's still a story that's really popular so people must believe it at the same time as they don't believe it.'

'Mickey,' says Miss Hurley with a beaming smile on her face. 'I think you have just made a major advance in your study of literature. You may have a credit.'

I'm a bit confused. I wasn't meaning to make a major advance in the study of literature. I was meaning to make a major advance in my case.

She hands over the piece of gold paper that means that Newman will be happy on Monday morning.

'Have a wonderful weekend, Mickey,' she says. 'I know I will. It's not often as a teacher that you leave school on a Friday afternoon thinking you've taught someone something.'

She puts her bag over her shoulder and sweeps out of the classroom.

I can't bring myself to tell her that I haven't the faintest idea what it is she thinks she's taught me.

But what I've learnt from the guy who wrote Little Red Riding Hood is that it's always worth trying to get away with impersonating someone else. And if I'm going to solve this case then I could do with being someone else in about an hour. And the person I need to be is George Martin – the killer bee competition winner.

The thing is though that if I want to be George Martin then I've got to make sure that the real George Martin is out of the way. Nothing is guaranteed to blow your cover more successfully when you're impersonating someone else than the real person suddenly turning up. Red Riding Hood would never have believed that it was really her grandmother in the bed if she'd seen her outside in the garden planting flowers a minute before she went into the cottage with her basket of provisions.

The wolf stuck Little Red Riding Hood's grandmother in a cupboard but there's no way that I could do that to George Martin so I'm going to have to come up with something else. Something that will stop him appearing at the radio station at five o'clock and meeting Girl Power.

'Oi! What are you doing?'

I look up. It's one of the school cleaners. I'm still sitting at my desk even though the pips have been gone for about ten minutes. It's no wonder he's suspicious.

'You kids,' he says. 'Spend all day chucking sweet wrappers on the floor and then you're too lazy to even get up off your backsides and go home. I suppose you want me to call you a cab, do you?'

'What?'

'You heard. I said I suppose you want me to call you a taxi. The youth of today. I despair, I really do.'

I leap out of my chair.

'A taxi is almost a great idea,' I tell him. I grab my bag and rush for the door.

'Oi!' he shouts after me. 'I was only joking. That's the trouble with you kids. All litter and no sense of irony.'

I sprint down to the bike shed, unlock my bike and pedal like crazy to get home as fast as I can. All the way there I'm praying that my sister isn't using the phone. I ride up to my house, jump off my bike and run to the hall. I'm lucky. The phone is free.

I need to ring Directory Enquiries to get George Martin's number. I put my hand on the receiver but before I can lift it, it rings. I pick it up quickly.

'Hello,' I say.

'Hello,' says a Scottish woman's voice. 'My name is Lorraine and I work for Universal Applications Limited and I wonder if I could speak to the householder for a minute.'

That's the last thing I need.

'No,' I tell her, 'You can't'

'It would only be for a few moments and it would allow me to bring to your notice a number of fantastic offers which the company is running at the moment for a limited time only.'

'No thanks,' I say.

'We could make you tremendous savings on your gas bill.'

'No.'

'And your electricity bill.'

'No.'

'And we will offer you an extremely low price on a brand new conservatory.'

'No, no, no!'

'Or a stylish new kitchen.'

I'm never going to get this woman off the phone.

'Or double glazing. If you have the front of the house done then we will do the back for free.'

'We don't have any windows,' I say. I need to get this woman off the phone so I can make my call.

'We could put the windows in for you,' she offers.

'We don't have a house,' I tell her.

'We could build you one,' she snaps back.

'We don't want one. We live in a field.'

'We have an excellent range of lawnmowers.'

I slam the phone down. Why didn't I think of that before? Then I pick it up again.

'We also do tents and caravans,' says the Scottish woman.

'I put the phone down on you,' I shout at her.

'You're a very rude person,' she tells me. 'But we'll forget it if you agree to put your name down for a lifetime commitment to two weeks in a luxury apartment block in Majorca which is currently under construction.'

What can I say? I've got to get her off the phone.

'All right,' I say.

'This phone call is being taped and a verbal contract is binding,' she says. 'Do you understand?'

'Yes,' I say.

'A representative of the company will contact you in a few days to finalise the details,' says the woman. 'Goodbye.'

The phone goes dead.

'Who was that?' shouts my dad from the lounge.

'Wrong number,' I yell back. I don't think this is the time to explain to him that we'll all be going on a lot more foreign holidays.

I dial Directory Enquiries. The way my luck seems to be going everybody in Abbey Road will have the surname Martin.

I'm wrong. There's only one. I dial the number and do some coughing to try to get my voice to go deeper. I hear the ring tone. Don't squeak, I say to myself. Whatever you do, don't squeak.

'Hello.'

It's a boy's voice.

'Hello,' I say. 'This is Johnny Feegan of Bubble FM. Can I speak to George Martin, please?'

'I'm George Martin.'

'Good. Congratulations on your victory in our competition.'

'Thanks.'

'Killer bees. A great answer. How did you know?'

'I guessed.'

I can't believe it. I did a whole load of research to be sure that my answer was right – well, okay, I asked my dad – and this kid gets a lucky guess. And he wins the competition. The world is a very unfair place.

'My mum was going to drive me down to the radio station in about a quarter for an hour. I can't wait to meet Girl Power. They all look wonderful.'

'Don't come,' I say.

'What?'

'The thing is,' I say, 'That you're right about Girl Power being so wonderful. And do you know what they are going to do?'

'What?'

'They're going to send a limousine to pick you up from your house so that everybody in your street knows that you've won a competition.'

'Wow!' yelps George Martin. 'A limo! For me!'

'That's the sort of special people that Girl Power are,' I tell him. 'The limousine will be leaving the radio station any second now so if you wait outside your house then it will be picking you up soon.

'Wow!'

'Oh what's that,' I say, pretending someone is talking to me. 'I'm just hearing from our traffic reporter that there's a hold up on the way to your house.'

'What?' says George. 'Should I get my mum to drive me then?'

'Absolutely not,' I tell him. 'Girl Power want you to arrive in a limo and they'll be prepared to wait for you. They think you're that important. So you just wait in your street for as long as it takes. Nothing will start until you're here.'

'Wow!' he says again. 'This is the best day of my life. I'm going outside to wait right now.'

The phone goes dead.

I know I should feel guilty. I've just ruined the best day of that kid's life and he hasn't done anything to deserve it. But I haven't got the time.

I decide to spend twenty minutes feeling guilty tomorrow when I shouldn't be so busy.

CHAPTER 22

'I'm George Martin,' I tell the receptionist. 'I won the competition to meet Girl Power.'

'You'll need a name tag,' says the receptionist.

While she's writing my name on a tag I check out the reception area for Bubble FM. There are massive photos of all the presenters stuck on the walls. They've all got these cheesy grins and look like they're always having a really good time. Which is probably why I get fed up listening to the radio after a bit, because it doesn't seem to matter what presenter you listen to they always seem to be in the same mood as the last one. And that mood is cheerful and happy and ready for a good laugh. It gets a bit boring after a while. What I'd like is that after you'd had a cheerful presenter for an hour you then got a grumpy one who was having a really bad day. That would be loads more interesting

'You need to clip this on,' says the receptionist handing over a name tag. 'Johnny's producer will be out here any minute to get you.'

'Thanks,' I tell her.

'Your name tag's upside down.'

'Oh.'

I try to clip it on so that the name is the right way up but every time I let go it falls upside down again. The receptionist stares at me the whole time I'm doing it.

'It won't stay straight,' I explain after my third attempt.

'There's nothing wrong with my name tags,' she snaps back. 'I've been on a course.'

'George Martin?'

I turn round. A large woman has just come through a door at the back of the reception area. She's got a big smile on her face and is holding out her hand. I offer her mine and she shakes it really hard.

'Welcome to Bubble FM. I'm Debbie Doyle, Johnny's producer. Do you know what a producer is?'

Without waiting for me to answer she explains.

'A producer is a person who handles the show's running order, screens the calls from listeners and who has a strategic overview of the show's direction.'

She puts her arm round me and moves me towards the door she came through.

'Now what we're going to do is this. Johnny is doing an interview with Girl Power right now. And what I think would be fantastic was if we just took you straight through to the booth and introduced you to the girls on the air. It's spontaneous, it's fast, it's cheeky, it's now. You know what I mean?'

I haven't got a clue what she means. She leads me into a room with three spotty men sitting at computers.

'This is the newsroom,' she tells me. 'Now are you okay about going straight on the air?'

I open my mouth to say no.

'Of course you are. All you have to do is to be natural. Be yourself and you'll be fine.'

The one thing I can't be is myself. I have to be George Martin.

'Over there is the booth. Can you see Girl Power? I'm going to give Johnny a sign and we're going to go straight in.'

This is all happening a bit quickly. I'm not that sure that I'm ready.

'Er...' I begin.

'Don't say "er",' Debbie tells me. 'It's bad radio. And don't cough or sneeze. You don't have a stutter, do you?'

I shake my head.

'You'll be brilliant. Ten seconds and we'll be going in.'

Suddenly I remember something very important. Girl Power all saw me yesterday. If they recognise me then they'll just call for Peter Peterson, their security guy and I'll be chucked straight out.'

'And let's go.'

She pushes me up to the door of the radio booth, reaches round to open it and then pushes me in.

Johnny Feegan and Girl Power all ignore me.

'Johnny,' says Debbie, 'this is George Martin. He won the competition to meet Girl Power.'

Johnny looks up from behind this big desk with loads of knobs and buttons on and nods at me for about a millionth of a second. Girl Power, who are on the other side of the desk, carry on eating pizza.

'Sit there by the microphone,' says Debbie pushing me to the nearest chair. 'And, remember, be yourself.'

She shuts the door behind her. Everybody in the sound booth carries on ignoring me. Johnny's headphones are sitting on the desk and through them I can hear the tinny sound of Girl Power's single.

Not one member of Girl Power has looked at me yet so I still don't know if they'll recognise me.

Johnny Feegan puts his headphones on as the song begins to fade out.

'That was great, that was grand, that was Girl Power,' he says. 'As you know, listeners, the girls are here with me right now and so is one lucky boy. Yes, George Martin the winner of last night's competition, the boy who knows more about killer bees than anybody else, is here in this booth with us right now. George, say hello to Rachel, Kim, Susie, Mel and Desiree. Otherwise known as Girl Power.'

Suddenly everybody's looking at me. Loads of questions rush through my mind at once. Do they recognise me? What's my name supposed to be again? Where do killer bees live? What was it that Johnny Feegan just told me to say?

'Aaaah, I think he's shy,' says Rachel.

I don't think any of them remember me.

'And what boy wouldn't be shy with five babes like you in the booth?' says Johnny. 'I'm blushing myself and I'm old enough to know better.'

He pauses like he's waiting for one of them to say that they don't think he's that old but they don't which isn't that surprising. Wearing big red glasses doesn't hide the fact that he's bald.

'So, George,' says Johnny amicably, 'What do you like most about Girl Power?'

They all look at me. I try not to look back and stare at the microphone instead. This interview thing is much tougher than you think.

'Er...' I say.

'Just spit it out,' says Johnny encouragingly.

'Say what's in your heart,' says Rachel.

'Yeah,' says Kim, 'Just put it out there.'

'You're one of our fans,' Mel tells me, 'And we're just so grateful to meet you.'

'We never forget that our fans put us where we are,' says Susie.

'Er...' I say again. Why can't I think of anything? 'I

like the fact that they are girls and I...er...like the fact that they...er...have...power.'

I sound like such a moron.

'I like powerful women too, George' says Johnny Feegan cheerily. 'But by that I don't mean women who are strident and unpleasant but women who recognise that their power lies in their femininity. Women like Girl Power who are excellent role models for young females everywhere because they're always focussing on the positive.'

'That's right,' says Rachel. 'We're just putting positive energy out there for people and if they can get with the vibe then they're going to be keeping it real.'

'And,' says Kim, 'When we get to meet people like George...'

'Special fans like George who we're so glad can be at our concert tonight,' interjects Mel.

'Then,' says Kim. 'Then we just know that what we're doing and all the stuff we have to go through is worth it because it's not about the fame.'

'Or money,' says Susie.

'Or glamour,' adds Rachel.

'What's it about then girls?' asks Johnny.

'The music,' they all say together.

'And that's the note on which we've got to end our all too brief visit from Girl Power, ladies and gentlemen. We'd love to talk more but they've got a concert to do tonight which I'm sure George is looking forward to, aren't you George?'

He looks at me. I nod. He looks annoyed.

'Nodding doesn't make for very good radio, George,' he says.

'Oh,' I say.

'Bye-bye, Girl Power,' he says.

'Bye, Johnny,' they all chorus back at him and then the five of them walk out of the studio.

Without me.

'Hey,' I shout. 'Don't forget me.'

'George,' hisses Johnny. 'We're still on the air.'

'So?' I hiss back. 'I'm not coughing, am I?'

And then before he can say anything else to me I'm out of the booth.

I catch up with Girl Power as they're going through the newsroom. Debbie Doyle is showing them out.

'Stop,' I shout.

Debbie Doyle stops so Girl Power have to stop too.

'Don't forget me,' I say. 'I'm George. I just won the competition to hang out backstage with you and go to your concert tonight.'

'Do we really have to go through with this?' says Rachel to Debbie.

'Yeah,' says Kim. 'He's been on the radio now. Why can't we just dump him?'

I think they're talking about me. They're nowhere

near as friendly as they were on the radio. In fact you'd think they hated me.

'Girls,' says Debbie. 'I agreed with your manager that if Bubble FM committed to saturation play of your single then you would spend the hour before your concert with George. If you don't agree then the deal is off.'

'I suppose we'll have to do it then,' sighs Kim. She turns round to look at me. 'But don't talk much, okay, George?'

I shake my head.

'Good,' says Rachel. 'Keep it that way and we'll all be happy.'

Debbie Doyle leads us into Bubble FM's reception area. Standing by the receptionist's desk looking big and menacing is Peter Peterson of Peterson's Personal Privacy Protection. I take a deep breath. If he recognises me then there's a good chance that I'm going to find myself face down in another puddle.

He turns round. I look down.

'Ready to go, girls?' he says.

'Yeah,' says Kim. 'This boy is coming with us.'

'Has he been vetted?' demands Peter Peterson.

'No,' Susie tells him.

'Then he can't come with us,' says Peter Peterson. 'He could be a stalker or a terrorist.'

'Or both,' says Debbie Doyle.

'Vet him now,' says Rachel.

'I can't do that,' says Peter Peterson. 'I need to give his name to a contact of mine in the police who will feed it into the vast terrorist and stalker database to see if we have a match.'

'Look,' says Mel. 'He needs to come with us if this radio station is going to play our single so sort it out. Okay?'

'I suppose I could do speed-vetting,' says Peter Peterson doubtfully, 'though as your Personal Privacy Protection Provider I must caution you that I advise against it.'

'Just do it,' says Kim.

Peter Peterson grabs me by the arm and pulls me away from the band.

'Look at me,' he says.

I look at him hoping that I won't see his eyes register any kind of recognition. Because if they do I'm in trouble. He's got me by the arm so I wouldn't even have the chance to run.

He doesn't say anything for a second. Then his eyes narrow suspiciously.

'Have I seen you before?'

This isn't good.

'No,' I tell him.

'Are you sure?'

'Yes.'

'Are you a stalker or a terrorist?'

'No.'

He lets go of my arm.

'Congratulations. You've successfully passed the vetting procedure. Let's go.'

I follow him over to the girls.

'Let's go to the limo,' he shouts. 'If we don't head over to the Colosseum now then the roads will be blocked with your fans' traffic and we'll risk being late.'

He leads Girl Power out through the revolving doors. I'm about to follow them when the receptionist shouts, 'STOP!'

I turn round.

'Give me back my name tag,' she says.

I sprint over to her desk and throw it down. As I turn back I bang into a boy who's running to the desk.

'Get out of my way,' he says.

I don't bother to argue. If I don't catch up with Girl Power before they're all in the car there's a good chance that they'll leave me behind.

I head for the door. Behind me I hear the boy pleading with the receptionist.

'You've got to help me. Somebody has stolen my identity. I'm the real George Martin.'

That revolving door really spins as I charge through it.

Mel is pulling the door of the limousine shut behind her. I sprint over and grab the handle.

'What the...?' she shouts. 'Oh it's you. You'd better get in.'

I get in. All five members of Girl Power are already in there. Peter Peterson is sitting in the front.

'Let's go,' he tells the driver.

The car starts.

I take a second off from thinking about the case to ask myself one brief self-indulgent question. How many other boys are at this moment sitting in a car with five good-looking girl pop stars? None that I can think of. But I am. That makes me pretty cool.

'What are you looking at?' says Kim.

'Er...' I begin. I didn't realise I had been looking at her.

'Don't drool over me,' she tells me.

'Or me,' adds Susie.

'No one would drool over you,' says Mel. 'The VJ on MTV said you were fat.'

'He said you were spotty,' snaps back Susie.

'I have sensitive skin. It's better than greasy hair.'

The thing is that actually being in a limousine with five girl pop stars is never going to be anywhere near as good as imagining being in a car with five girl pop stars. Reality is always a let down.

They all get out their mobile phones and start making calls. But even in the back of a big limousine there isn't enough space for five people to have phone calls so they start talking louder and louder until I feel like all their voices are zooming round inside my head and banging off the sides of my skull.

Which is not helping me think. But I try harder and somehow I manage it. Since I've found myself with Girl Power I've discovered a good thing and a bad thing. The good thing is that Desiree never says anything and looks miserable. That means that there must be a chance she might miss the Really Tough Crew and want to hang out with them again. The bad thing is that since I've discovered that she's joined Girl Power I've been so obsessed with getting past their security and getting to her that I haven't bothered to think about what I'm actually going to say when I get there.

We pull up by the stage door to the Hanford Colosseum.

'Girls,' says Peter Peterson. 'We've got to go in now. I've scanned the area for threats and can confirm that if we move swiftly I can virtually guarantee your successful arrival in the backstage area though I would like to make it plain, in case of future lawsuits, that even a dedicated professional like myself can never promise one hundred percent security.'

'I want my own dressing room,' shouts Kim. 'I need peace and quiet, away from these selfish and bitchy remarks.'

'If she's getting her own dressing room then I want one too,' yells Mel.

'So do I,' screech Rachel and Susie.

'I'll go and ask,' says Peter Peterson.

He's back real quick with the manager of the Colosseum.

'I'm afraid it's completely impossible,' the manager tells them.

'I'm not going on if I don't get my own dressing room,' Kim tells him.

'Neither am I,' says Mel.

'Or me,' says Rachel.

'Or me,' says Susie.

Desiree doesn't say anything.

The manager looks at them to see if they mean it. They do.

'Maybe it is possible after all,' he says.

CHAPTER 23

'What about me?'

Girl Power are about to disappear into their five different dressing rooms which, despite being completely impossible for the manager to find five minutes ago, are now all free and available.

'You're not getting your own dressing room,' the manager tells me. 'You aren't in Girl Power. You're not even a girl.'

'I know that,' I tell him. 'But I've won a competition to hang out with Girl Power for an hour before the concert and I don't see how I can do that if they are all in separate dressing rooms.'

'Maybe you could hang out with each of them for a fifth of an hour,' suggests Peter Peterson.

'That's a great idea,' says the manager. 'What is a fifth of an hour?'

'Twelve minutes,' says Peter Peterson.

'That was fast,' observes the manager.

'Mental arithmetic is one of my hobbies,' explains Peter Peterson.

'I don't want him first,' says Rachel. She goes into her dressing room and slams it behind her.

'Neither do I,' say Kim, Mel and Susie who all go into their dressing rooms and slam the doors behind them.

I look at Desiree. She shrugs.

'I'll call you in twelve minutes time,' says Peter Peterson.

I follow Desiree into her dressing room. I can't believe how lucky I just got. Finally things are beginning to work out my way.

As soon as the door closes behind us I know I've got to start talking. I've only got twelve minutes to talk her out of the band.

'How long have you been in Girl Power?' I ask.

She sits down and looks out of the window.

'Too long,' she says.

That's a good start.

'The other girls don't seem too nice,' I hint.

'They're bitches.'

This is getting better.

'I don't think your single's that good,' I risk.

'It's a piece of manufactured junk. None of the others can sing. Mine is the only real voice on it. They had to put all theirs through computers. Even when we're live mine is the only microphone that's switched on.'

This is going really well.

'I heard you were in the Really Tough Crew before,' I say.

She looks surprised.

'How come someone as sad as you has heard of the Crew?'

I decide this isn't a good time to get offended.

'I heard they were excellent and that they stood a really good chance of getting a record deal,' I tell her.

'We weren't too bad,' she says and there's the faintest hint of a smile on her face.

'But without you the Crew won't get anywhere. Everyone says you were the most crucial part of their sound.'

'I was pretty good,' she agrees.

'I'm sure they're desperate to have you back.'

'Do you think?'

'I'm certain.'

'Mmmm,' she says and I can tell she's thinking about it. There are times when you've said as much as you can and you've just got to keep quiet and leave people to make up their own minds. This is definitely one of those times.

I keep very quiet for a couple of minutes. Every second that she thinks about it is bringing her closer to rejoining the Really Tough Crew. But if I'm going to get her to the recording studio in time for the big session this evening then she's got to make a decision soon. I give her one more minute to convince herself and then I say,

'So, what do you think?'

'What do I think about what?' she demands.

'About rejoining the Really Tough Crew?'

'What?'

'You were just thinking about it.'

'No, I wasn't. I was thinking about what to do with my first million. If our single goes top five in at least six countries in Europe then I'll be a millionaire by next year.'

'But what about making real music with the Crew rather than the rubbish you said that you sing with Girl Power?' I protest.

'Listen,' she says. 'I've made it. I'm a star. In a year's time I'm going to be very rich and very famous. I'm not giving all that up just because the songs aren't that good.'

'But...' I say. 'But...but...'

And then I shut up. I keep saying 'but' but I can't actually think of one. What a fool. Thinking that someone would give up being rich and famous just for a bit of musical integrity.

There's a knock on the door.

'Your twelve minutes are up,' says Peter Peterson.

As I walk out of Desiree's dressing room I know that I'm beat. The recording session starts in less than an hour and there is no way that I can get Desiree out of the band by then.

'It's Rachel next,' says Peter Peterson.

I shrug. I feel like telling him to forget it but if I did he might get suspicious. I can't suddenly change from being Girl Power's biggest fan into someone who couldn't care less about them.

'Good,' I say.

'You don't sound like you think it's good,' says Peter Peterson. 'I don't understand you. A chance to be with your favourite pop stars and yet your mood seems so low.'

I try to look enthusiastic but I don't think I manage it. It's not an expression I use very often so I'm probably a bit out of practice when it comes to faking it.

It certainly doesn't convince Peter Peterson. He just shakes his head and opens the door to Rachel's dressing room.

She's sitting in front of a mirror staring at herself.

'Sit down and shut up,' she says. 'I don't have no time for you at all. Just because I have to spend twelve minutes with you does not mean that I have to speak twelve words to you. That's it. I have make-up to put on.'

I'm tempted just to walk straight out. I mean I've known rude people in my life but this is rudeness on a whole new level. This is celebrity-rudeness. But if I did I'd be doing exactly what Rachel wants so I sit down. Maybe if Peter Peterson was in this room now he'd understand why I feel so low.

So low.

Something goes ping inside my head.

Solo.

What always happens to manufactured girl bands and boy bands? They have a few hits but after a year or so they can't stand each other any more and they split up and all say they're going to have solo careers. Every one of them ends up this way. And it gives me an idea. It's not a nice idea but it's an idea that might work and this is no time to get choosy.

'I don't know whether I should tell you this,' I say to Rachel.

'Then don't,' she says. 'I do not have the time to hear that my music has changed your life and I'm the most gorgeous girl you've ever seen.'

'That wasn't what I was going to say.'

'Didn't you hear me?' She bangs her hairbrush against the mirror. 'I don't want you to talk to me. I am preparing myself to give a superb performance. I need to focus.'

I take a deep breath.

'I suppose you'll want it to be a really special performance because it'll be your last one.'

She stops brushing her hair.

'What are you talking about?'

'Desiree's leaving.'

'What?'

'I heard her on her mobile. She was talking to

someone. It was a journalist, I think. She was saying something about being sorry to leave you other girls behind but she needed to move on to the next stage of her career.'

'What?'

'I couldn't hear what the journalist said but from what she was saying there will be a front page story tomorrow announcing her solo career.'

'The bitch.'

I can't believe it. She's buying it.

'I'm going to kill her.'

She stands up. So do I. I run over to the door and block it.

'No,' I say.

'Get out of my way,' she says and she raises her hairbrush in the air.

'You can't let on that you know,' I say.

'I can do whatever I want.'

She slashes at me with the hairbrush and I have to duck.

'No, you can't,' I say.

This time I pull my head back just in time as the hairbrush whizzes past my nose. Sooner or later my luck is going to run out and she's going to connect.

'You can't tell her because if you do then she'll know that you know and she's already got her story out there which means that she'll get the successful solo career.'

I duck again.

'It's the law of manufactured pop bands,' I explain. 'Only the first one to leave gets a successful solo career. Think of Robbie. Think of Beyoncé. Think of Justin. What happened to all the others? They never had another hit record. What you've got to do is to go solo before Desiree does.'

She's about to swipe at me one more time but she changes her mind. What I've just said has had an impact.

'But how?' she says. 'She's already rung a journalist and got her story in the paper tomorrow. How can I leave before that?'

She's got a good point there. According to my story it's going to be impossible for Rachel to get herself officially out of the band before Desiree does. Inside my head I call myself an idiot for not saying that I'd heard Desiree tell the journalist that he couldn't use the story for two days. Then there would have been a gap. Then my plan would have worked.

'You're not saying anything,' points out Rachel.

Typical. Five minutes ago she was telling me to shut up so she could focus and now she's having a go at me for not saying anything.

'You can't think of anything, can you?' she says.

I beg my brain to come up with an answer.

'I'm going to see Desiree,' she says. 'No way can she do this to me.'

'No,' I say.

It's all going to fall apart.

'Get out of my way.'

'I know how you can beat her.'

'No, you don't. I think she might be your favourite after all and you're protecting her.'

'No, I'm not,' I say, desperately backing into the door. 'You're my favourite. All the fans like you the best.'

This stops her for a second.

'Do they really?'

'Yeah...yeah.' Think, brain, think. 'They say that you've got the coolest look.' Come on, brain. 'And the best body.' Come on, brain, 'And...er...really nice...' There must be a way, 'shoulders.'

'Shoulders?'

'What?'

I'm trying so hard to think of a solution to the Desiree problem that I'm making mistakes when it comes to handing out meaningless compliments.

'You said the fans like my shoulders.'

'No,' I protest. 'I meant they like your shoulder length hair.'

'I haven't got shoulder length hair. Kim has.'

'Oh.'

I can see by her face that I've made the biggest mistake you can make with a member of an all-girl pop group which is to get her mixed up with one of the others.

'Now get out of my way before I scream.'

'What?'

'You heard.'

She opens her mouth.

'Tell the crowd at tonight's concert.'

I don't know where that came from but it makes her close her mouth.

'After the first song announce that it's your final concert because you're leaving the band to go solo. Then tomorrow all the papers will have stories in about how you left and when people see Desiree's story they'll think that she rushed it out afterwards because she was so bitter and that you were the one who left the band first so you're the one who'll get the best solo career.'

She thinks about it for a second.

'That just might work,' she says.

I breathe a sigh of relief so big that the carbon dioxide content of the room doubles. We did it in Biology. Oxygen goes in and carbon dioxide comes out. But they both look like air so you don't notice.

'Except...'

I don't believe it. After all my hard work there's an 'except.' I'm not sure my brain can cope with it.

She looks down.

'You see my microphone isn't always switched on.'

Oh no. I'd forgotten that.

'It's for technical reasons,' explains Rachel without

looking at me. 'You see my singing voice is so good that I'd show the others up so they won't let me sing. That's why it's so important for me to go solo. So I can show the world what I can really do as an artist.'

Oh yeah. So she can have all her vocals put through a computer so they sound in tune and then she can mime all the time.

'I know,' I say remembering what Desiree had said about her microphone being the only one switched on for real. 'Why don't you grab Desiree's microphone straight after the first song and announce you're quitting. She won't be expecting it.'

Rachel looks doubtful.

'Do you think that will work?'

'Definitely.'

'What if she won't give me her microphone?'

'Grab it,' I say. 'Grab it like you'll grab your first number one spot with your first solo single.'

'You're right,' she says. 'I'll do it.'

There's a knock on the door. Peter Peterson's head appears.

'Time's up,' he says to me. 'Next stop, Kim.'

'Thanks, George,' says Rachel. 'What you've told me has changed my life.'

'All in a day's work for your biggest fan,' I tell her.

'I'd kiss you,' she says. 'But you're not good-looking enough.'

'What did you say to her that was so amazing?' asks Peter Peterson when we get outside the door.

'It was something to do with a dance routine,' I say quickly. 'It's kind of technical.'

'Oh.'

He knocks on the door of Kim's dressing room and we go in. I wait for him to close the door and then I suck most of the oxygen into my lungs,

'Kim,' I start. 'I don't know whether I ought to be telling you this but you're my favourite member of Girl Power and I think you need to know what I overheard Desiree saying on the phone...'

CHAPTER 24

'LADIES AND GENTLEMEN.'

'I'd like to order a taxi please.'

'BOYS AND GIRLS.'

'Outside the stage door of the Hanford Colosseum.'

'IT'S THE MOMENT WE'VE ALL BEEN WAITING FOR.'

'Ten minutes time.'

'LET ME HEAR YOU MAKE LOTS OF NOISE.'

'Going to the recording studio on Penny Lane.'

'FOR THE ONE THE ONLY.'

'The name. The name is Mickey...er...George. George Martin.'

'**GIRL POWER**.'

I slam down the payphone in the backstage corridor. Simultaneously, five dressing room doors open and Rachel, Kim, Mel, Susie and Desiree step out into the corridor. None of them look at each other and none of them look happy.

The manager of the Colosseum rushes back from the stage where he's been introducing them.

'You're on, girls,' he shouts. 'Go for it.'

They push past him and head down the corridor towards the stage.

I follow them.

'George. Stop.'

I stop. Behind me is Peter Peterson.

'Aren't you supposed to be round the other side by now?' he asks. 'You've got a reserved front row seat.'

'I want to watch it from here,' I tell him.

'That wasn't in the prize, was it?' he points out. 'The prize was backstage before and front row during.'

I can't believe he's going to mess up my plan.

'Yes, but being here is so much more exciting,' I tell him.

'I'm not responsible for your excitement. I'm responsible for the Girl Power's safety. And to ensure their safety I need as few people as possible with access to them. Which means you should get round the front.'

'But I've been vetted,' I protest. 'You did it yourself.'

'I know,' he says. 'But it wasn't the full vetting. Now you be a good boy and run along to your front row seat. There's a little door just down the corridor. It'll take you less than a minute. Go on.'

'Just one song.'

'Now.'

I do not believe it. After all the hard work he really is going to ruin my plan. Everything is perfectly in place. I only need to stay here for three more minutes.

'Do I need to use force?'

I shake my head and walk to where he's pointing. I slide the bolt across and open the door.

A crash of noise hits me in the face as I look out at thousands of screaming kids. Peter Peterson shuts the door behind me. I wait a second and then push to see if it opens. It doesn't. He must have pushed the bolt back shut and slid away my last slim hope of success.

'Boy you got looks and money
And plenty of style
Let me be your girlfriend.
Let me make you smile.'

Girl Power's single booms out of the speakers as I head to my seat. Not that anybody's sitting down but I can tell which is my seat because it's the only one on the front row without a nine year old bouncing up and down on it.

It's right in the middle. I walk over to it and sit down.

On stage, Girl Power are doing the same dance routine that I saw on The Hits Show. It seems so long ago even though it's really three days. A lot has happened since then.

'I love you Girl Power,' shrieks a nine year old girl bouncing up and down on the seat next to me.

> *'Boy my day is wasted*
> *Unless I'm with you*
> *Let me be your special one*
> *Let me love you true.'*

Even though I know it's not possible, I try to work out how I might get to the stage. There's two sets of stairs, one on each side but two massive bouncers holding walkie talkies are blocking them. There's no way past.

> *'Boy I'll give you all my love*
> *More love than there could be*
> *Let me be your only one*
> *Let me make you see.'*

I should go. But something stops me. Even though I know that my plan can no longer work I have to see if it would have. I know I'm torturing myself but I have to know.

On stage Girl Power move closer to each other for the final chorus,

'Boy, though the sun and moon
Are falling from the sky
Tell me I'm the girl for you
And I won't even cry.'

They stop in their final pose and hold it for a second. All around me the nine year olds jump even higher and shout even louder. And then, exactly like I'd planned...

Everything goes crazy.

Rachel, Kim, Mel and Susie all make a grab for Desiree's microphone. Rachel bangs into Mel and Susie trips over Kim and stumbles into Desiree who falls backwards onto the floor. The four other girls jump on top of her.

The nine year olds stop jumping up and down and go quiet. This is not what pop bands are supposed to do.

Desiree somehow manages to get to her feet. She looks frightened and surprised which is understandable. Thirty seconds ago she was a pop star. Now it looks like she's a wrestler. She's still holding her microphone. That's what the other girls want but she doesn't know that. So she makes a run for it.

But she's too late. Mel dives forwards and grabs her round the ankles and sends her sprawling. Susie bangs Desiree's arm hard against the stage. Desiree's microphone spills out. Susie reaches out for it but Rachel sprints over and grasps it first.

'Everybody,' shouts Rachel, 'I just want to tell you that I'm leaving the...Ow!'

Kim has charged at Rachel and headbutted her in the stomach. The microphone flies out of Rachel's hands and lands next to Mel. She grabs it and sits up.

'I've got to tell everybody in the audience,' yells Mel, 'That because of musical differences I am...get off.'

But Susie doesn't get off. She yanks Mel's hair back until you think it's all going to come out.

'Drop the mike. Drop the mike,' Susie shouts at her.

Mel throws the mike across the stage. It lands next to Kim who quickly gets a hold of it.

'People,' she tells the audience. 'In order to fulfill my dreams as an artist I...'

Rachel grabs the mike back off her.

'I'm going solo,' she yells.

Kim pulls the mike back.

'No, I am,' she screeches.

Susie drags the mike away from her.

'I'm quitting the band,' she shrieks. 'And I did it before they did.'

'No, you didn't,' screams Mel as she dives on top of her. 'It was me.'

Kim and Rachel join in the fight. All of Girl Power are fighting each other now apart from Desiree who is, unfortunately for her, stuck underneath them while they battle it out.

I can't believe it. It's all working beautifully.

But I can't do the very last thing that will make the plan complete.

Peter Peterson appears on the stage. He looks worried. I don't blame him. When it's your job to ensure the personal safety of five members of an all girl band I suppose you prepare for everything except them attacking each other. From the front row, I see he isn't sure what to do. Then he says something into his walkie talkie. The two massive bouncers answer him. Then they start heading up on to the stage leaving the stairs unguarded.

It's amazing. Maybe I'm going to get a chance after all.

The initial shock of seeing the fight start has passed as far as the nine year olds in the audience are concerned. From all around me I hear shouts of, 'Go Rachel! 'Get her, Kim!' 'Hit her, Mel!' and 'Use your nails, Susie!' as they cheer on their favourite member of Girl Power in the fight. I don't hear too many yells for Desiree but then again she is face down on the stage with her hands covering her head so it's not as though she's giving the audience value for money.

The two bouncers run onto the stage. Peter Peterson points to the girls and shouts some instructions. All three of them pile into the pop star battle to try and pull the girls apart. The nine year olds in the audience start to boo.

This is my chance. I've got to go now. I get out of

my seat and run towards the nearest stairs. I climb them two at a time and sprint straight past the fight to where Desiree is cowering. I crouch down next to her.

'Hi,' I say. 'How are things going?'

She looks up.

'Why are they all attacking me?' she wails.

'Maybe they're jealous of your voice,' I say.

'Do you think so?' she asks. Jenni was right when she told me she was dumb.

'I don't know for sure,' I tell her. 'But what I do know is that we've got to get you out of here fast. It's not safe any more.'

This is the crucial moment. What's she going to do?

You can see she's not sure either. She looks at me and then she looks at the mess of bodies fighting on the stage.

Somehow a microphone flies out of the writhing mass and clunks against the side of her head.

It seems to make up her mind. She nods to me.

'Come on,' I say. I help her get up and we make for the backstage area. But at the edge of the stage she stops and takes one look back at the audience and the remains of her pop career that is scrapping with the bouncers amid the heartstopping cries of bloodthirsty children.

'It's not all glamour, you know,' she tells me.

'Come on,' I say, pushing her backstage. 'We've got to get you away from here. Everybody's gone mad.'

I look behind me. Peter Peterson looks up and sees me at the same time. He sees me pushing Desiree. Panic covers his face.

'Boys,' he shouts. 'It's a ruse. One of our pop stars is being kidnapped.'

He starts to run towards me. The other two bouncers pull themselves out of the fight and start chasing too. I don't wait around to see anything else.

'Run,' I shout to Desiree. 'They're all coming after you.'

Thankfully after what's happened to her in the last five minutes she'll believe anything bad about the rest of her group. She sprints ahead of me through the narrow backstage corridors.

'Stop!' yells Peter Peterson.

'Keep going,' I shout.

We whizz past their dressing rooms, dodge round the Collosium manager, streak down the long corridor, nip past the toilets, pound down the stairs and kick open the safety door.

Please let the taxi be there.

It is.

I put my head through the door.

'Taxi for George Martin?' says the driver.

I pull the back door open.

'Get in,' I tell Desiree.

She gets in. I'm about to follow her when from nowhere something grabs my arm. It can't be Peter Peterson. He hasn't come through the stage door yet.

I turn round. It's a kid about my age. I've seen him somewhere before.

'You're not George Martin!' he yells. 'I'm the real George Martin and I'm performing a citizen's arrest on you for stealing my identity.'

'Get off!' I shake my arm but his grip gets tighter.

'I'm the real George Martin,' he repeats.

'All right,' I tell him. 'You can have your identity back. I don't want it any more.'

'I don't want my identity back now,' he yells. 'I wanted it earlier today when it was fun. You've stolen the best day of my life.'

'It was a rotten day,' I tell him. 'They're all horrible and they can't sing.'

'I don't believe you,' he says. 'Girl Power love their fans.'

I don't have time to argue with him because just then the stage doors crash open and Peter Peterson and the bouncers spill out. The noise distracts George just long enough for me to pull myself free and throw myself into the cab.

'Drive,' I yell at the taxi driver.

I'm still pulling the door shut as the taxi starts to move. There's a bang on the top as Peter Peterson tries to stop the car.

'He's denting my roof,' says the taxi driver indignantly. He jams his foot to the floor and we accelerate until Peter Peterson is just a little suit in the distance.

CHAPTER 25

It's only five minutes to the recording studios. Neither of us says anything the whole way there. We're both trying to get our breath back and I'm checking my watch to see how late we are. It was fifteen minutes when we got in so it's twenty minutes when we stop at the studios on Penny Lane. I hand over the fare to the driver.

'Let's go,' I say to Desiree.

'What?' she says. 'Who are you to give me orders? If this is where you're getting off then fine. I'm taking this taxi home. I miss my dog.'

I remember that dog. I can't figure out how anyone could miss it.

'Nobody's taking my cab anywhere,' says the taxi driver. 'I've got a pick-up from the station. Everybody's getting out here.'

'Thanks,' I tell him. He's saved me explaining everything to Desiree. I don't want her to know what's going on until the very last moment.

The two of us are left alone on an empty street. I feel rain start to fall on my head.

'So?' says Desiree. 'What do we do now? We need a cab and I left my mobile at the Colosseum because we left in such a rush.'

'I haven't got a mobile,' I tell her. 'But if we go in here,' I nod towards the recording studio, 'I'm sure they'll help us out.'

'You know,' says Desiree, 'I really don't understand what was going on at the Colosseum. Maybe I should talk to the other girls and find out.'

'Let's just go in here,' I say quickly. The last thing I want is Desiree trying to make sense of what has just happened. She might succeed and then I'd be in real trouble.

She follows me in through the doors looking puzzled. When we get in there I hurry over to the reception desk and say as quietly as I can.

'We're with the Really Tough Crew.'

'Studio B,' says the guy behind the desk. 'You're late. They've already laid down the rap.'

'Thanks.'

I turn round to Desiree.

'The man says we've got to go to Studio B,' I tell her.

'But there's a phone there,' she says pointing at an unnecessarily big red phone on the receptionist's desk.

'The man said we've got to go to Studio B,' I repeat.

I head towards Studio B. Desiree looks even more confused but she decides to follow me. I'm just grateful that she's as dumb as Jenni said she was. But even she's going to catch on to the fact that something is up when we get in there.

The red light outside the Studio goes out just as I get to the doors. I pause for one tiny microsecond, smile at Desiree and pull them open.

Inside Studio B are Jenni, the rest of the Really Tough Crew and Jenni's little brother DJ Smarty and some guy with glasses who I don't recognise. I figure he must be a producer or an engineer or something.

They all look up when I walk in. It's my moment of glory. I move aside and they can all see Desiree.

Unfortunately, that means Desiree can see them which makes my moment of glory more like half a moment.

'What's going down here?' she demands.

'Hi Desiree,' says Jenni, taking off her headphones and walking up to us. 'Hi, Mickey.'

That's Jenni's first mistake.

'Mickey?' screeches Desiree 'I thought your name was George?'

'George?' says Jenni. 'I don't understand. It said Mickey on his detective advert. Still I don't care what his name is if he can bring you back here to rejoin the Crew.'

That's Jenni's second mistake.

'What?' shouts Desiree. 'Rejoin the Crew? I'm not here for that. I'm here to get a taxi home.'

'What do you mean?' protests Jenni. 'You're supposed to be here to sing your vocal.'

'Hey?' says Desiree.

'Now,' insists Jenni.

'Perhaps we should all calm down,' says the producer guy.

'Shut up,' say Jenni and Desiree together. For no reason at all I notice that they shout at him in different tones so it comes out like a harmony. The producer guy goes back to his board and twiddles nervously with his knobs.

'George,' says Desiree. 'What is going on here?'

'Yes, Mickey,' says Jenni. 'What is going on?'

Everybody in the studio is looking at me.

'Isn't it enough that everybody is back together and now we can all live happily ever after?' I ask.

'No,' says everybody in the room. Even the producer guy and it's not like it's any of his business.

'This isn't a book,' points out Desiree who is really quick on the uptake. 'This is real life. Now tell me what is going on.'

'Right,' I say. 'It's like this. Are you sitting comfortably?'

'Get on with it,' snarls Desiree.

I've got to make this good or I could blow the whole case.

'You see I'd always been a fan of yours, Desiree, and I know what great work you'd been doing with the Really

Tough Crew but then I saw The Hits Show and I realised that you'd left them and gone to join Girl Power. So, I became a Girl Power fan but really I was just a fan of yours and I was desperate to meet you so I entered the competition and I won. And then when I was with the other girls I overheard each of them planning to attack you and steal your microphone and announce they were going solo. They'd each got this idea that only the first member of a manufactured band to leave ever has a successful solo career. I don't know where they got that idea from. Anyway I was going to warn you but I didn't have time because Peter Peterson made me leave the backstage area. All I could do was watch in horror while you were attacked and, as soon as I got a chance to rush on to the stage and help you to safety, I did.'

I stop. I don't think that went too badly.

'But?' says Desiree.

Maybe I thought too soon.

'Yeah,' I ask.

'That explains why you saved me. That doesn't explain what we're doing here.'

'Doesn't it?' says Jenni, who's caught up with the fact that if Desiree decides that there was any kind of big plan to get her here she won't sing.

'No.'

There's a silence. Everybody keeps looking at me. I wonder if they can hear my brain humming as it tries to come up with an answer.

'It's like this,' I tell Desiree with a smile. Always look confident when you're lying. 'I'd kept up with what was happening to the Really Tough Crew after you left even though I knew that they wouldn't be anywhere near as good and I knew that they'd got this recording session audition tonight. And then when I discovered what the other girls in Girl Power were planning to do I knew what you had to do to save your pop career.'

'You mean develop it, don't you?' hints Jenni.

'Oh yeah,' I nod. 'That's right. Develop it. You see with Rachel, Kim, Mel and Susie all going solo there's going to be way too many ex-Girl Power singles out and everybody will be slagging them off and saying that they're sell-outs. But you, Desiree, you'll be different.'

'Will I?' asks Desiree.

'Yes. Because you'll have gone back and rejoined your own Crew. You'll be coming straight from the Hanford Hood instead of out of some sell-out record company and so you'll have credibility with the kids. Everyone will say that Desiree's the only one keeping it real.'

I daren't look at Desiree to see if what I've said works. I can't believe I got through the bit about 'keeping it real' without laughing.

'You might be right,' says Desiree.

I think I've pulled it off.

'Of course he's right,' says Jenni. 'Now let's do your vocal.'

'Except...'

I don't believe it. First there was a 'but' and now there's an 'except'.

'Why are you calling him Mickey when his name is George Martin?'

'Mickey Sharp is his name,' explains Jenni.

'No, it's not,' insists Desiree. 'It's George Martin and I'm not singing until I know why he's got two different names.'

'Oh,' says Jenni. 'Well, Mickey?'

'Or George,' interjects Desiree.

'You'd better explain to Desiree why you've got two different names because then we can get on and record her vocal.'

Inside I can feel myself sagging. After the last few days I don't know whether I've got enough energy to come up with one last explanation. Why do I have two names when I don't? It's a good question and I don't have a good answer. Unless...

'I don't have two names,' I say.

'Hey?' snaps Jenni.

'What?' demands Desiree. 'Mickey Sharp and George Martin just aren't the same. That's what I've said and there's no way you are going to tell me different.'

'I didn't say they were the same,' I tell her. 'I said they were both my name.'

'You aren't making sense,' says Desiree.

'Yes I am,' I tell her. 'I told you I was desperate to win that competition on Bubble FM right. Well that competition said that you had to say where there were the most killer bees in the world. Now I knew the answer was either Mexico or Brazil but I wasn't sure which one because the thing with bees is that they can fly. So they could be in either Mexico or Brazil. And I didn't want to risk getting it wrong so I rang in both answers. I said I was Mickey Sharp for Brazil and George Martin for Mexico because I'm both. My middle names are George and Martin. My full name is Mickey George Martin Sharp.'

I try not to look too relieved to have got my explanation out. I just hope Desiree goes for it.

'We haven't got much time to record your vocal,' says the producer guy.

'Come on, Desiree,' says Jenni. 'Sing.'

Desiree gives me a long look. I stare right back at her. After what seems like an hour but is probably ten seconds she shrugs and walks over to the studio microphone.

'You got the backing track ready?' she snaps at the producer. 'I'm a star already, you know, not like everybody else here, so I don't want to be kept waiting around. I want to sing.'

I slump down into the nearest chair.

Case closed.

CHAPTER 26

It's the day after the recording session and I'm sitting in my shed with the newspaper.

'GIRL POW! BASH! BIFF! BANG! WALLOP!

We're used to bands battling on The Hits Show but not like this. Young children watched in horror on Friday night as top pop idols, Girl Power, went crazy right in front of them. Chaotic scenes broke out at the Hanford Colosseum after only the first song of the night when for no reason four of the band Rachel, Kim, Mel and Susie attacked the fifth member, Desiree, and then fought amongst themselves. They were only separated after the intervention of Peter Peterson of Peterson's Personal Privacy Protection who exclusively told this reporter, 'When the people you're protecting start attacking each other it's a real dilemma for the professional protector.' All four girls involved in the attack have since announced solo careers. However an industry insider said, 'They'll never have another hit after all that violence. Their images are irreparably damaged.' He added, 'Desiree won't be hurt by this though. The public will be sympathetic because she was the one attacked and she's also the only one not to launch a cash-in solo career on the back of it.' However Desiree's whereabouts remain a mystery. She was last seen being led off the stage by a mystery boy. There are rumours that this was her new boyfriend but this correspondent thinks this is unlikely as the boy in question just wasn't good-looking enough. All the children who witnessed the horrific scenes have been offered counselling.'

I slam the paper down. I was really enjoying reading the article until that line about the boy not being good-looking enough. I was on the stage so the journalist must have been much too far away to tell how good-looking I was. And there was strobe lighting as well which can easily confuse people. So he shouldn't have written it.

The shed door opens. Umair walks in.

'She's coming,' he says.

I nod.

'This had better work,' he says.

Katie Pierce saunters through the open door and leans against the side of the shed. This being the weekend she's even better-looking than normal. She really can take your breath away. The thing with Katie though is she wouldn't give it back.

'Hi Katie,' I say.

She looks around the shed.

'So,' she says. 'This is where you hang out. The shed in my garden has got useless tools and creepy crawlies in it.' She looks at me and Umair. 'So, not much difference there then.'

'Good to see you too,' I say.

'I got your message,' she says, 'And I was free due to an unexpected curtailment in my social schedule. And I've never been to this part of Hanford before. Apparently you've got electricity now.'

'Have you just come here to insult me, Katie?'

'Mickey,' she turns her big brown eyes on me. 'Even insulting you is more of my attention than you deserve.'

'Thanks for making the extra effort then.'

'What can I say?' she shrugs. 'I'm a generous girl.'

'Good,' I say. 'So maybe you'd like to do a deal?'

'A deal?' she says. 'What have you got that I could possibly want? You're not offering me your body, are you?'

Even before I can tell myself not to I know I'm going red. She gets me every single time.

'You were offering me your body!' she says.

'Forget about my body.'

'I'll try Mickey though it may reappear in my nightmares.'

This situation is getting away from me fast.

'What I want to talk about,' I say, 'Is the sudden unexpected curtailment of your social schedule. I think we may be able to help you there.'

She shakes her head.

'Mickey, it's not because there aren't boys queueing up to take me out. There's been a little misunderstanding, that's all, which has resulted in me being temporarily grounded. I really don't need your help.'

'Something to do with Hanford Cemetery?'

She loses her cool for a second.

'What did you say?'

'You heard,' I tell her. 'I know that you were arrested in Hanford Cemetery for messing with graves.'

'Don't be stupid,' she snaps, 'You've finally lost it, Mickey.'

'You know how I know?'

'I don't know what you're talking about,' she says.

'I know, because Umair here just happened to be wandering through the graveyard at Friday lunchtime and he was a bit tired and he decided to have a little sit down behind a gravestone.'

Katie's stopped talking now.

'And do you know what he happened to see?'

'No.'

'He saw two boys who he couldn't recognise messing about with a shovel and some earth. And then a girl appeared and she saw the boys messing about and because she was a really nice girl she got angry and chased them off. Then she picked up the shovel and said very loudly, "I must take this to the gravedigger and then report this matter to the police". But who should appear just at that moment but the police themselves. And, believe it or not, the police thought that the girl was the one in the wrong. And they took her away instead. Now, Umair could have stopped them at the time but he thought that the police might wonder what he was doing there so he remained hidden. But his conscience has been nagging at him and he feels that he must go to the police and tell them the truth. Which is that the nice girl is completely innocent.'

'Who's stopping him?' says Katie. 'He can go down to the police station right now.'

'Of course he could,' I say. 'And I know that he would if he didn't have these other worries.'

'What other worries?'

'About his missing diary. The diary I asked you to bring along when I left my message.'

Katie shakes her head in disgust. But it's fake disgust. She knew what was coming all right. The only question is whether we've got a deal. I don't know how tough the police have been on her and how angry her mum is about it all.

'Mickey,' she says, 'I'm really sad that you and Umair could sink so low.'

'Only as low as you,' I point out. 'You were quite happy to get me arrested.'

Katie shoots Umair a dirty look.

'You betrayed my confidence then?' she says.

Umair nods. We've agreed that only I'm going to do any talking until the deal's done. That way she can't try to set us against each other. When Katie's in a corner she can twist almost anything.

'What can a girl do?' sighs Katie. 'Boys let me down every time.'

'What can you do?' I say. 'Apart from hand over the diary.'

Katie sighs one more time. A really big sigh that seems to sum up her massive disappointment in the male sex that has acted so deviously against her. Part of her even believes it too.

Then she pulls out Umair's diary from her bag and drops it on my desk.

'There you go, Mickey,' she says. 'Now I can go down to the police station with Umair and watch him go in and make his statement. And then I'm going to sue for wrongful arrest.'

I chuck the diary over to Umair. He stands up to go off to the police station with her.

All of a sudden I get a bad feeling. There's something about Katie that's wrong. I've known her a long time and

I know when she's still got one last ace up her sleeve.

'Katie,' I say quietly. 'I'll take those other pages if you don't mind.'

'What other pages?'

'You know what other pages. The one or two you ripped out to give you a chance to take revenge later on.'

'Mickey, you're taking advantage. You can't go back on the deal now you've got the diary.'

'Give me the other pages, Katie.'

'I don't know what you're talking about.'

'The other pages, Katie.'

'There aren't any.'

'Umair can check the diary before he goes. To see every page is really there.'

She doesn't say anything. She's still got her back to me so I can't see what her face is doing. Maybe she doesn't have any more. Maybe she was being straight with us. I decide to count to ten and see.

I get to nine when she whips her hand into the back pocket of her jeans, pulls out two torn pages, spins round and slams them on my desk.

'All right,' she hisses into my face. 'You've got it this time. But this is not over. Do you hear me? This is not over.'

I nod. Now it feels right.

'Come on you,' she snaps at Umair. 'And make sure you make this statement good. Nothing like your lousy poetry.'

And she wheels round and storms out of my shed.

Umair gives a rueful smile and follows her.

I decide to enjoy the moment. I pull out a can of coke and a packet of salt'n'vinegar. I'm one step ahead of Katie. For now. But I know it won't last. She'll be back. And worse than ever.

Still that's for the future and all I've got to worry about now is munching on my crisps and wondering if I can cut out this newspaper article as a souvenir without getting the 'not good-looking enough' bit in.

'You're looking very pleased with yourself.'

I look up. Standing in the doorway is Jenni.

'Am I?'

'Trust me.'

She walks in and sits down on the box. I hope there are no splinters sticking up.

'I didn't believe you were going to do it,' she says. 'But you did. Of course it would have been better if you could have brought her back a bit nicer. She's still vain and selfish and petty.'

'Hey,' I say. 'I don't do personality changes. I just do finding people.'

'Chill,' she says holding up one hand. 'I was just joking.'

'Oh,' I say. 'Right.'

'And she may be vain and selfish and petty but she's still got that voice. I don't know whether we'd have got the deal without her.'

'You got a deal?'

'Yeah,' she says. 'It's only a development deal to start off with which means that they give us studio time and pay our living expenses but it's a whole lot more than we had yesterday.'

'Congratulations,' I tell her.

'Like I said, I don't think we'd have got it if it wasn't for you, Mickey.'

'So you won't do that rap about me letting people down at your next gig?'

She shakes her head.

'Nobody will ever hear that rap again,' she says, 'Which is a shame because it was kind of catchy. But it wasn't real. And that's what counts. You don't let people down.'

I smile. People don't normally say nice things about me.

'Now down to business,' she says, pulling some notes out of her pocket and plonking them on the desk. 'There's your fee. We even threw in a bonus because you managed to split up Girl Power as well as putting Desiree back in the Really Tough Crew. That's two services to music for the price of one.'

She stands up to go. After the good things she's said I don't want her to.

'Hey,' I say very quickly before I can think about what I'm saying and go red. 'How about you and me getting together and hanging out some time?'

'You and me?'

I nod. I've got the words out. I can't say any more until I know her answer.

'Mickey,' she says. 'There are some people that you meet and you only know them for a little while. And in that time they do such impressive stuff and you think such good things about them that you don't want to see them again, because you think so much of them that the only way that they can go in the future is down. So you've got to learn to say goodbye and leave it. That's you and me, Mickey. So, I've got to go.'

She smiles and walks over to the door of the shed where she turns round.

'But I'll blow you a kiss during our first TV appearance.'

And with that she's gone. And I know like you sometimes do that I'll never see her again. And I know that one day she'll be on the TV and I'll be watching.

I lean back take a swig of coke and wonder about what she said. Did she mean all that stuff about everything being so impressive that you have to let it go or was she just saying no politely?

I eat three bags of crisps and drink two more cans of coke thinking about it, but when my mum shouts me that it's tea time, I still don't know the answer.

THE END